DEADLINE

BOOKS BY THOMAS B. DEWEY

The "Mac" series:

Draw the Curtain Close
Every Bet's a Sure Thing
Prey for Me
The Mean Streets
The Brave, Bad Girls
You've Got Him Cold
The Case of the Chased and the Chaste
How Hard to Kill
A Sad Song Singing
Don't Cry for Long
Portrait of a Dead Heiress
Deadline
Death and Taxes
The King Killers
The Love-Death Thing
The Taurus Trip

The Pete Schoefield Series

And When She Stops
Go To Sleep, Jeannie
Too Hot For Hawaii
The Golden Hooligan
Go, Honeylou
The Girl With The Sweet Plump Knees
The Girl in the Punchbowl
Only on Tuesdays
Nude in Nevada

The Singer Batts Series

Hue and Cry
As Good As Dead
Mourning After
Handle with Fear

Others Novels

My Love Is Violent
Hunter at Large
Can a Mermaid Kill?
A Season of Violence

DEADLINE

THOMAS B. DEWEY

WILDSIDE PRESS

CHAPTER 1

Peter Davidian was twenty-two years old. That's young to die. But Peter Davidian, barring a last-minute miracle, surely would die within a week. He would die the bad way, in a steel chair wired with enough voltage to light up a good-sized town, with his head shaved and his pants legs slit. They say you don't feel it, but at twenty-two I guess you feel it now and then while waiting.

It was a bad year for miracles. The kind Peter Davidian needed hadn't occurred since the raising of Lazarus. His lawyer, Sam Birch, who knew all about the differences between private eyes and miracle workers, nevertheless laid it out for me in very clear terms.

"The kid is going to go," he said, "unless we can dig up some mitigating circumstances in the next day or three or four."

"Mitigating…?"

"You may well ask," he said. "But it maybe isn't so dreamy as it sounds. There's a group behind us."

"Sure there is," I said. "Twelve jurors, a prosecuting attorney, and an electrical engineer."

"All right, but let me give you a little background. The nature of the crime made the verdict practically inevitable. I mean, it was the crime that got judged, more than the man who did it. So my psychiatric defense didn't get off the ground. My client could have sat there in a strait jacket, foaming at the mouth, they still would have thrown him the big one. So—what we have to do is convince the governor that to execute this kid would be a miscarriage because of his provable emotional incompetence. And I think we got ways to prove it—that I didn't have at the time of the trial."

"What about this group you mentioned?"

"Good group—doctors and psychologists and a couple of lawyers. Very prestige, impeccable and, I might add, enthusiastic. They got a big drive and they like this case."

"Well—but what's their nudge? What do they get?"

Sam shrugged.

"So they're do-gooders. I don't know what they get, but I don't really give a damn, if I can get my client a commutation."

I kept quiet. Nothing against do-gooders especially, but the whole thing felt funny to me.

"Oh—they've got funds," Sam said, with a trace of slyness.

"I'm glad," I said. "Everybody ought to have money."

"Which is how I'm able to call on you. My client hasn't got a nickel and he doesn't know anybody with a nickel."

"This is some kind of test case or something for them?"

"Now you're on the stove," Sam said. "Exactly. They like the rough ones."

* * * *

It was a rough one.

After leaving Sam in his office, I drove west and south for about two hours until I came to a country town called Wesley. It was in farming country and that was all they had there, farming and a few stores and services on a short main street. There was a hotel named the Clark House. It had been built fifty-five years ago by a man named, and the ancient, ponderous man at the desk could easily have passed for the original proprietor. He was white. That is to say, the hair he had left was white, his eyebrows likewise, and his skin was turning white, so that in certain lights parts of his face and head sometimes disappeared while you were looking at him.

He was friendly, though. I wrote my name and address in a book and he gave me a key. He asked how long I thought I would stay, and I said I couldn't be sure, probably three, four days. That was fine with him. The only name on the register page I had signed was my own. At a glance it appeared that, aside from a slender old gentleman nodding over a newspaper in the front section of the lobby, I was the sole tenant of the Clark House. Because there were thirty rooms on three floors, that made for a high vacancy factor. Still, the white old man at the desk didn't seem discouraged. His sense of humor was as sturdy as the pale bones in his round skull. As I turned from the desk he said:

"Hope it'll be quiet enough for you."

At the back of the lobby, where the stairs began, a broad double door was barred with a plank nailed in at both sides. On the plank a yellowed sign read: closed. Above the doors, in fading gold letters, was the legend: DINING ROOM.

In the old days, I thought, launching myself on the climb to the second floor, they would come to the hotel for Sunday dinner. One dollar for all the fried chicken, mashed potatoes and gravy, and peas and carrots you could eat, with apple pie and coffee for dessert. Was it better then?

The second-floor hall was so dark I had to pause and blink six times before I could spot the numbers on the doors.

Whether it was better then, I thought, I don't know. But I may find out. I'm back there now—except that the dining room is closed.

My room was on the front side, Number Eight. The key worked easily in the lock, too easily.

Have to fix that, I thought. And then I thought, Cut it out with worrying. You're in the country now.

I raised the window shade and put my suitcase on a straight-backed chair beside an authentic brass bed. It had two mattresses on a set of sound springs, hair underneath and down on top. The room was clean. There was a washbowl with a mirror for shaving. I looked out and down the hall and at the near end, on a door that stood slightly ajar, read the words: toilet and bath. I closed the door, wishing vaguely that the dining room were open for business.

From the window I could see the far side of for its entire length, except for a couple of buildings at the west end. One of them, I learned soon, was a feed-and-grain store and the other a filling station. There was another filling station at the east end of the street. In between were stores—dry goods, hardware, grocery—a bank called the Farmer's and Merchant's National Bank, and a restaurant called the Wesley Café. There wasn't much pretense in Wesley. Everything was labeled with rock-bottom fitness.

The label on the barnlike structure opposite the bank and across a narrow, paved street that came to a dead end at was in three parts:

INTERNATIONAL HARVESTER
JACK PARRISH
SALES—RENTALS

I looked at the establishment for some time. Not that I'm fascinated by farm machinery, but the hard-core reason for my presence in town was that eight months before, Peter Davidian, according to the local county court records plus the records of all the available higher courts up to the U.S. Supreme, had assaulted, murdered, and mutilated a girl named Esther Parrish, age eighteen. The man who had the tractor and farm-machinery franchise in Wesley would be Esther Parrish's father.

* * * *

It was three in the afternoon, the street was full of sunshine, and there was nothing that could be accomplished in the hotel room. I opened the suitcase and got out the thick file in the manila envelope that Sam Birch had given me earlier that day. It was a considerable file. In addition to the highlights of the trial testimony, there were voluminous, detailed reports of psychological and psychiatric examinations of Peter Davidian and a comprehensive study of the case made by the group that was so determined to save Davidian's life. Also, it was paying my wages, rather liberally, in fact, and among other items in the file was a list of local names and places that bore on the crime and the trial. It was my job to develop what I could about the personality and habits of Peter Davidian and of some others, including Esther Parrish, along with any hitherto neglected or obscured circumstances that might, if known, throw an altering light on the situation. I had never had such a job before, and it was hard to be hopeful. A list of names is a piece of paper with words on it. I would have to breathe life into it, and time was short.

I put the list in my pocket, shoved the rest of the file in the envelope, replaced it in the suitcase, and started to leave the room.

A startled female voice squeaked: "Hey!"

In the dimness of the hall I made out a slender woman in a white summer dress and a pair of serviceable-looking glasses, not unattractive on her. It was easy to see that when I had opened the door, it had come within millimeters of hitting her in the high, slightly turned-up nose.

"Excuse me," I said.

She gave me a look and adjusted her position to make up for the displacement caused by the opening of the door.

"Didn't mean to almost hit you in the nose," I said.

She gave me a look and looked away.

"It's not the nose so much," she said, "but the glasses cost forty dollars."

"Then it was a lucky save."

She nodded, turning away. I went back into the room and closed the door, starting over. While I was giving her a couple of seconds to get where she was going and disappear, I thought about the file. I opened the suitcase, got it out, and stuck it under my arm.

Country or not, I thought, you never can tell, and it's the only file I've got.

I opened the door and almost broke her glasses for the second time. She was headed in the opposite direction and she had a towel over her arm.

"My goodness," she said in a neutral tone.

"Honest," I said, "I'm not trying on purpose to bug you. I forgot something and had to go back for it."

She glanced at the thick envelope under my arm and it seemed to give her some confidence. She smiled a little. She was quite pretty around the mouth and she had that cute nose. Her eyes were somewhat hard to evaluate because of the glasses.

"It's just that until now," she said, "I thought I had the hotel all to myself. I'm not used to the traffic problem."

"Well," I said, "I'll only be here for a few days."

"I hope you enjoy your stay," she said.

She smiled again politely, turned, and walked rather primly down the hall toward the toilet-bath.

Down in the lobby, I asked the alabaster desk clerk whether I could store my envelope in a safe place.

"Well," he said, "we got a safe here. It's old, but it ain't been broken into for fifty years, and I guess it's as safe as the next one."

"That's safe enough," I said.

I wrote my name on the envelope, licked the flap, and stuck it down.

The safe was off in a corner and he went over there, stiff on his legs, bent, and started monkeying with the dial. It didn't take him long to open it. He had to bend a little farther to put the envelope inside, and he halted suddenly and his white old face looked up over the desk into the lobby.

"Hey, Walt!" he said.

The old codger, napping over the paper, turned his head slowly.

"Yeah, Jess?" he said.

"Did Miss Adams come in? I was out for a spell."

"Yeah. She come in a few minutes ago. Went upstairs."

"Carnsarn," Jess said, and finished laying away my file. "Got a special delivery come in for her and I put it away, didn't see her come in."

He came away from the safe.

"That tight enough for you?" he asked.

"That's fine," I said. "You mentioned Miss Adams," I added. "Would that be Miss Vivian Adams, from Chicago?"

"Nope," he said. "'Twouldn't."

"Oh," I said.

I thanked him and headed for the street, thinking that if I wanted to know more about Miss Adams, I'd have to find somebody more talkative than Jess.

After the cool dark of the hotel the sunlight on the street was fairly dazzling. I walked west, past the store fronts I hadn't been able to see from the window because they were directly underneath, on the same side with the hotel. I passed a five-and-ten, a dry-cleaning plant, and a drugstore. It gave me a sense of security to note that the drugstore contained a soda fountain. Between it and the café across the street, I'd be able to get nourishment.

Between the drugstore and the next building was a vacant lot, and then came the town hall. It was a three-story building with a square bell tower. Stairs led up at one side to a meeting room on the second floor. The chambers of the town council were on the third floor. One half of the ground floor was a firehouse with the doors open and the big red wagon facing the street. The other half was occupied by the town constable and the jail. That was my first stop.

The constable's name, according to my list, was Roscoe Embers. He had been the first official person to view the body of Esther Parrish, though he had not made the discovery. There was a way-out chance that he knew more than he had ever let on, but a much better chance that all he knew was that it had been a sorry sight and a crying shame.

I found him behind a desk piled with long-outdated bulletins and communiqués from the sheriff's office, in a cubbyhole of an office so cluttered it must have been quite a trick for him to open and close the door without spilling. He was in his sixties, puffy around the waist and in the face, and he had abnormally small hands, almost a girl's hands. But the rest of him was male enough. He was writing laboriously with a dull pencil and the tip of his tongue was sticking out from one corner of his mouth.

"Be right with you," he said, without looking up.

I waited for him to finish—standing because there was no clear chair to sit on—and it didn't take long. He got his tongue back in his mouth, sagged back in his swivel chair, and waggled his bushy brows at me.

"Goldarn paper work, drive a fella crazy," he said.

"I know how it is," I said.

"What can I do for you?"

You have to start somewhere. There's no way I know of to go into a small town looking for information and keep it a secret.

"I'd like to talk to you about the murder of Esther Parrish," I said.

It gave him quite a time. He moved around in his seat and picked up the pencil and tossed it down again, looked over his left shoulder at a barred door which, by way of a vanishing corridor, led into the jail, and scratched at the back of his neck with one little hand.

"Well, now," he said.

"Any time," I said, "but it would be better now."

He straightened himself out some.

"Who would I be talking to?" he asked.

"Me," I said. "It's a public matter, I think. I mean, the thing was reported, there was a trial and all that."

"Yeah," he said, "but if it isn't official, you know, I've got a lot to do around here—"

"It's official. I'm representing an attorney."

"Oh," he said, with some relief.

It didn't seem to make any difference which side I was on, but I couldn't be positive of that.

"You're the one who reached the scene of the crime first, I understand," I said.

I didn't understand anything of the kind, but it was proper to follow protocol.

"Well, not the very first. I was with the posse we got up. I looked at the poor girl and around the place some, waitin' for the sheriff's people to get there."

"How did it look?" I asked.

"It was a sorry sight," he said. "Young girl like that—a cryin' shame."

So we had got past that part of it.

"What time of day was it?"

"Night—after ten—about ten-thirty."

"How come the posse? What got it started?"

"Oh—well, you know—" His eyes snapped suddenly. "Why d'you ask? Girl had disappeared. Her father was upset. Everybody wants to help—"

"I understand," I said.

Along in there I began to lose him. Everybody hates to reopen a closed issue, and peace officers seem to hate it more than others. If he had played a notable part in tracking down the criminal, Embers might have been glad to discuss it. Apparently he hadn't.

"I can see you're busy," I said. "I won't keep you. Maybe we can talk about it some other time."

He shrugged and waved one of those miniature hands.

"Few more days," he said, "there won't be nothin' much to talk about."

He had reference to Peter Davidian and the electric chair, and I didn't like the tone of his voice. I nodded, found the doorknob, and let myself out onto the street.

I had Fred Sampson and his wife on my list, but according to my vague conception of rural life, there wouldn't be anybody home at four in the afternoon. They'd be out in the fields somewhere. The time to go visiting on the farm, I decided, would be in the evening after the chores were done.

I walked back to the drugstore and sat down at the soda fountain. The place was deserted except for a tall guy in a white jacket behind the prescription counter, a bulky woman in a street dress bustling around the cigar counter, and a lanky, oddly misshapen fellow in a sweat shirt and dungarees who was earnestly mopping the floor. He was pretty good at it except that he put a lot more muscle into it than was necessary. He had the down-cast, furtive expression of a retarded personality and his mouth was busy nearly all the time, making words nobody could hear.

Probably a free-lance writer, I thought, who finally found a steady job.

The woman came to the fountain and served me a coke. I asked wheth-er a girl named Mary Carpenter still lived in town and whether she ever came into the drugstore.

"Oh, sure, Mary's around," the woman said. "You acquainted with her?"

"No—I'd like to talk to her."

"I see."

She did a little bustling with a bar rag over the immaculate imitation-marble counter.

"If it's about Esther Parrish and all that," she said, "I doubt if she'll talk to you."

"All right," I said. "I'm not pushing it."

She finished with the rag, tossed it down, and went back to the cigar counter.

"Can't say I blame her," she said, going away.

I sipped at my drink, hearing the swish-swish of the mop on the lino-leum floor, the occasional banging sound as he dunked it in the bucket and brought it out.

"Say, Chris," the man in the white jacket said.

"Yeah?" the floor mopper said.

By way of the mirror over the back counter I saw the one called Chris cock his head, listening. But he didn't look up or pause in his chore, only worked a little faster and harder.

"How many chickens did Ferd Wiley say were in that last batch at the hatchery?"

"Two eighty-six," Chris said. "They was a hundred and seventy-eight yellow and a hundred and eight white. Started hatchin' Tuesday mornin', seven-thirty."

I swished the ice around in my glass to loosen it, tipped it up, and drank it. The druggist was making a note on a slip of paper.

Two hundred and eighty-six chickens, I thought. Seven-thirty Tuesday morning. That's good remembering.

The mop was splashing and swirling in the vicinity of my feet. I turned on the stool, lifting my shoes so he could work up against the facing of the counter. He didn't look at me. He was mumbling something. It didn't make any sense to me till I caught the name "Mary Carpenter."

"…Mary's seventeen, goin' on eighteen," he was saying. "Birthday comin' up September fourth. Esther Parrish was older—close friends though—real close. Esther was eighteen three days before she got killed. Gave a party—nice party—ten kids…" His voice faded as he moved away, mopping along the base of the counter.

I looked at my watch, paid for my drink at the cigar counter, and walked to the hotel, not too fast. I had a feeling of being followed.

In the lobby the old codger with the newspaper was gone and Jess the desk clerk was sitting on a black leather divan, dozing. I found a seat by a window and got out my list. There was nobody on it named Chris. I moved over to the divan and Jess blinked his white brows at me.

"Don't want to disturb you," I said, "but I'd like to make a telephone call—Chicago."

"Chicago?" he said sleepily.

"That's right. There's no phone in the room."

He heaved himself up to his feet and headed for the desk.

"Used to have phones," he said, "but got too costly. Have to be payin' that service charge every month whether anybody's usin' 'em or not."

"I understand."

He hauled up a telephone from under the desk.

"Welcome to use this one," he said. "I'll put it on your bill."

"Thanks."

I took out my list and laid it beside the phone and Jess started away behind the desk.

"Ran into an interesting fellow," I said.

"That so?" he said.

"Fellow named Chris, works at the drugstore."

"That's Chris Duval," he said. "Yeah, he's a character."

He went away and I dialed the local operator and placed a call to Sam Birch. Jess had gone the full width of the lobby and sat down with his back to me, looking out the window, as if to give me privacy. Sam Birch's answering service came on and said he was out and it might take some time to reach him. I said that there was quite a lot hanging on it and I would wait.

The hotel register was lying on the desk within reach. I opened it and leafed through it backward, page by page. My own name was the only one entered as of the current day, which was August 27. There were no entries for the three previous days, then there was an entry for a man named "Sam Bellow."

Some business, I thought.

One week and three days back there were two entries. One was a man-and-wife combination by the name of "Lineacre"; the other was a "Miss Caroline Adams."

I glanced at my list and closed the book. Half a dozen names down the list was a "Caroline Adams: high school teacher, 28. Knew Esther Parrish, Mary Carpenter and, presumably, Peter Davidian. Subject: English. Teacher in Wesley for three years—Consolidated Union High School on county road four miles west of town."

Sam Birch came on. He sounded out of breath.

"No report yet," I said. "Been here two hours. There's no mention in the file of a guy named Chris Duval."

He repeated the name. There was a silence.

"I've got the stuff right here," he said. "Hang on—yeah, there was a fellow by that name. Mental defective. I talked to him. He's got this fabulous memory for details. But he can't read or write. Because he's classified incompetent, there was no way to permit him to testify. But I don't know that he knew anything helpful. Why do you ask?"

"I don't know. The memory thing, I guess. He remembers when Esther Parrish's birthday was and how many people she had to the party, and the same about Mary Carpenter—maybe he remembers something else."

"Always possible. But don't pin too much on it. Anything else?"

"No—"

A whispy sort of presence in a summer dress came to the bottom of the stairs and walked briskly across the lobby toward the street.

"Got to go now," I said. "A girl just went by and I'd like to get a date."

"Mac!"

"A schoolteacher named Caroline Adams," I said.

"Oh—then good luck," he said, and hung up.

I hung up, waved thanks at Jess across the lobby, and headed out, following Caroline Adams.

CHAPTER 2

I caught up with her in front of the drugstore, where she was talking with Chris Duval. He was leaning on his mop handle and she was leaning on one hip, dangling a small purple handbag. The sunlight flashed off and on from her glasses.

Having caught up with her, I avoided the appearance of being on the chase by nodding pleasantly and entering the store without breaking stride. I bought a package of razor blades at the cigar counter, asked the bulky lady the time of day, and by that time Chris Duval had turned into the store and Miss Adams was on her way down the street.

I caught up with her again, carrying my small purchase in plain sight. There seemed to be something comforting to her in my having something in hand, maybe because it indicated that I really did have something to do besides following her around and opening doors in her face.

"Miss Adams—" I said. "There was a special delivery for you at the hotel. I happened to be at the desk—"

She unsnapped her purse, reached in, and came up with an envelope, folded once.

"I know," she said. "I picked it up. Thank you very much."

She had me on the run, more or less literally. She walked with a long stride and I had to open my own to keep up with her. It was like trying to make a date with someone who's pulling out on a train.

"Well, I'm glad you got it," I said.

"I also picked up the information," she said, "that you asked whether I was Vivian Adams of Chicago."

"I see—"

"Is there anything else you'd like to know?"

"Yes, there is, but it's not especially personal. I have the personal facts in hand."

"Indeed?"

"You are Miss Caroline Adams, a high school English teacher at the Consolidated Union High School on the county road four miles west of town. You're twenty-eight years old and you've been teaching school in Wesley for three years."

She didn't say anything for a minute, just walked a little more briskly.

"What do you want?" she said finally.

"I beg your pardon?"

"Obviously you want something from me. What?"

We had reached the town hall and she stopped, inclining toward the open door where the stairs went up. "I want to talk to you," I said.

"Well…" She looked at a small watch strapped to a slender wrist. "I have only a couple of minutes."

"Not enough."

"What do you want, I keep asking. Information?"

"Not exactly. I want opinions, reflections, appraisals—"

"You're taking some sort of survey?"

I took a deep breath.

"You could call it that, stretching it a little."

"Whom do you work for?"

"For a young man, twenty-two years old, who is going to burn to death in a few days unless I can find a reason why he shouldn't."

Her eyes left my face and her mouth tightened, then relaxed. Her eyes returned.

"Peter Davidian," she said.

"That's right."

"Are you an attorney?"

"No. I represent an attorney."

"Peter's attorney?"

"Yes, ma'am. Sam Birch."

She left me again with those eyes behind the glasses. Her mouth moved a little and I thought she was going to say something, but then it clamped firm again, she turned abruptly, and started up the stairs. I stood there in the sun and felt guilty because it wasn't burning.

Miss Adams made four steps on sharp, determined heels, then stopped. She stood quite still for the space of thirty seconds, then turned and came down again. She looked up at me and took off her glasses. Her eyes were mainly green, with an amber halo around each pupil, and, unobscured now, they were extremely intense.

"Listen," she said, "there isn't anything I can do for Peter Davidian. I wasn't a witness to anything. I was perfectly willing to testify at the trial, but I wasn't a witness to anything and there was nothing helpful I could say. I don't want to talk about the case to you or anyone else. It was very distressing to me and it still is. Please don't ask me again."

She turned away.

"Maybe, if you change your mind," I said, "we could have dinner—"

"That's impossible," she said. "There's a meeting tonight, a school meeting, with the board and some teachers and parents, and I'm in charge of the arrangements."

"All right," I said. "I'll keep hoping."

"You might save some time," she said, "if you don't." This time she went upstairs all the way and out of sight. I left the doorway and started off toward the west, where the street dwindled to open fields. But the setting sun was in my eyes and after a few steps I crossed the street and started back in the other direction.

I turned into the Wesley Café for a cup of coffee. It had a counter on one side, a row of booths on the opposite wall, and long rectangular tables down the middle of the room. There were half a dozen people, five men and one woman, at the counter, and I joined them. Nobody paid any attention to me except for a momentary glance.

The coffee was rich and hot. It was the best thing that had happened to me since hitting town, and I savored it fully. The conversation around me was loud and local. I couldn't make head or tail of it and that gave me a welcome sense of isolation. I didn't belong here. The assignment was hopeless and everybody knew it.

Thing to do, I decided, is to get through that list and look over the town, make a report, and get out—save the client's money.

There was Peter Davidian to think about, but it was unpleasant to think about him—as Miss Adams had said—and he was old enough to take care of himself.

Just barely, I thought.

Then the coffee was all gone and there was nothing to do but hit the street again. The sun was nearly gone, but there was plenty of light. We were heading into one of those long, late-summer twilights. There was more foot traffic on the street than there had been an hour earlier, most of it in and out of the grocery and drugstore, made up chiefly of women.

I walked up toward the bank, stopped at the alley alongside the big tractor and implement place, and looked it over. There were display windows on the street but no entrance. That would be around the corner, off the alley. In the showroom was a tractor about the size of a Sherman tank, shiny red and yellow. Aside from it, there was nothing on display except for a couple of small items I couldn't identify. For all I knew, they might be lawn mowers, but they didn't look exactly like lawn mowers.

At the back of the large room was an office beyond a glass screen. A spindly woman in rimless glasses on a drop chain was operating an adding machine. That I could recognize.

As I watched, a tall, thickset guy entered the showroom from the alley and went to the office window. Following him, almost running to keep up, was a slight fellow in overalls and one of those high-peak caps with a long bill. The bigger one wore a blue denim shirt, open at the neck, and a fat cigar. Everything about him was big, including his mouth, and it handled the cigar with precision and relish. The little one had some papers in his hand, and when they got to the cashier's window, the big one took them away from him and shoved them in to the lady in the glasses. The smaller guy stood there and waited.

The big one didn't have much time. He did some talking to the cashier and some to the little farmer. When he talked, you could see how he used the cigar for punctuation—up, question mark; one side, comma; down, period. He never touched it with his hand and he never lost it.

When he'd had his say, he walked out and the small guy stood at the cashier's window and waited patiently for her to finish. I didn't see any money change hands in either direction.

I went around the corner and up the alley to the main entrance. There was a wide driveway off the showroom and a long, open service area. Business didn't seem too brisk, but I learned later it was the harvest season and everything that would run was out working, not sitting around in the garage.

In one of the service compartments a battered pickup truck was up on a hoist and two mechanics were working underneath it. It was another case of Mutt and Jeff. One of them was almost as big as the one with the cigar and the other was skinny and short, fragile in his greasy coveralls. You could tell who was in charge by the height of the hoist. It was just right for the big fellow, too high for the shorty. He had to reach up, straining at every move. Consequently he wasn't very efficient.

There was no sign of the one with the cigar. Evidently he had had even less time than I'd thought.

The big one under the car came out and I walked over there. He was pretty well greased up and thus indistinguishable from a million other guys who hang around garages. Although big, he was muscle-bound and here and there larded, and he had the build of a gorilla with short, thick legs and wide shoulders. His arms were abnormally long.

"Looking for Mr. Parrish," I said.

He was wiping his arms and hands with a red rag and he didn't take any notice till he had finished and tossed the rag away.

"Ain't here," he said. "Gone for the day."

"Maybe tomorrow," I said.

I turned away.

"My name's Bledsoe," he said. "Tony Bledsoe. Anything I can do for you?"

I looked back at him. His name was on my list, but I couldn't recall the rundown on him.

"I'm kind of in charge when Jack's gone," he said.

"Thanks," I said. "No hurry. I'll be around tomorrow."

"Okay."

I started away again. I heard a hiss of air and then a raucous, obscene shout. When I looked around, Bledsoe had punched the release switch for the hoist and it was dropping, with the short mechanic still under the car.

By the time Shorty got out, he was on his hands and knees and small tools were clattering over the concrete floor where he had thrown them. Bledsoe hadn't made any move to stop the hoist. He was laughing. The little one got on his feet, brushing at his overalls.

"Kinda lowered the boom on you, huh?" Bledsoe said.

The small mechanic headed for the bench, muttering. He didn't offer to fight. It would have been ridiculous. I walked away down the alley, thinking they played rough in this little town.

But I guess there isn't much else to do, I thought then. Peter Davidian had found something to do, though, I decided. It had been a little rough too.

I crossed the street to the hotel and checked in at the desk. Jess was eating a ham sandwich and drinking coffee out of a thermos. There had been no calls for me.

"Looks like a good sandwich," I said. "Where did it come from?"

"Over to the Café," he said. "Pretty good."

He popped the last bite into his mouth and washed it down with coffee.

"Could I trouble you for that envelope you put away for me?" I asked.

"No trouble," he said. "No trouble a-tall."

He creaked over to the safe, opened it, and came back with the envelope.

"Look—uh—" he said. "I don't hardly ever ask questions—people come to the hotel, mind their business, leave 'em alone."

"I understand," I said. "Go ahead, ask me."

He glanced around the lobby, which was deserted except for the two of us. He leaned heavily on the desk and his white face hovered not far from mine.

"Word gets around fast in a small place like this," he said. "Are you lookin' into that—uh—murder? That boy Peter Davidian?"

"Yes, I am," I said.

"Well—which side are you on?"

"There's only one side interested in it," I said. "Davidian's."

He nodded and looked sad.

"Figured," he said.

I waited a short time.

"Was there anything else?" I said.

"No." He shook his head slowly. "Could I give you a piece of advice? Somethin' else I very seldom do."

"I wish you would," I said. "I can use it."

"Don't know if you can use this, but might save you some trouble." He leaned still closer and his voice dropped. "Folks are pretty touchy here about that," he said. "Seems like they're just waitin' for the boy to get executed so they can breathe easy and forget the whole thing."

"Well, I suppose so."

"And don't anybody want much to talk about it."

"I've noticed that."

"Like the town's kind of ashamed, you know?"

"I know."

"So I would say to you, one man to another—don't push 'em too hard. Feelin' still runs pretty high. You push 'em too hard, they get riled and it's nasty."

"Sure," I said. "I'll be careful. Thanks."

He nodded soberly.

"Only one other thing," I said. "It's kind of nasty sitting there on death row waiting for them to come for you—when you're twenty-two years old."

He nodded again.

"Reckon it is," he said.

That was all he had to say about that, and I left the hotel and went over to the Café to get a sandwich.

* * * *

I drove northwest out of town, heading for the Fred Sampson farm. There wouldn't be any problem about finding it. They had included a large-scale map of the town and vicinity in my file and every possible point of interest was clearly marked. The Sampson place was five miles out of town, and on the way, according to the map, I would pass the abandoned farm where Esther Parrish had been murdered. It was a small place, owned by someone back East named Donaldson, and nobody had worked it since Fred Sampson had given it up two years before. Peter Davidian had worked for Fred Sampson on both farms, for about two and a half years altogether.

* * * *

The death farm was a leaning barn at the end of a dry, deep-rutted lane. Once there had been a house, but it had burned down and only the jagged remains of the chimney showed black against the sky in the late, lingering twilight. There was a stretch of fence along the front lot, but it sagged badly and was overgrown with vines and ivy. I passed slowly, then drove on a mile and a half to the Sampson farm.

It was in good repair, though humble. A small house sat among fruit trees near the road. It had a forlorn kind of facade, sheared off, block-like, no porch, just the flat wall with some window holes in it. Beyond it, I made out a barn and some smaller buildings. A lightweight tractor was drawn up near the barn.

There were lights inside the house. I left the car on the road and walked up the lane to a door at the side, where the lights seemed brightest. Through the upper glass section of a kitchen door I could see a man and woman at a table, eating a skimpy dinner. Or supper. The woman was small and motherly-looking in a full gingham apron from the neck to the hem of her skirt. But there was nothing skimpy-looking about the man. He was in overalls; he looked to be around six feet four, and he looked more or less like Abraham Lincoln.

I knocked and they both looked at the door, then at each other for a while, and finally the man got up. It took quite a while because he had so far to go. It didn't take long for him to reach the door though. He had a stride of about eight feet. The really spooky thing about him was that he didn't say anything. He just opened the door and looked out—and down—at me and he didn't speak. It occurred to me that maybe he was mute because he couldn't help it, but I learned later that he could talk. I learned it within about half a minute, in fact. From behind him the woman said:

"Who is it, Fred?"

He turned his head to look at her and said the most logical thing possible at the time:

"I don't know."

He looked at me some more. There wasn't any question of whose move it was.

"I'm in town for a few days," I said. "Somebody told me you might give me some information about Peter Davidian."

"Peter...?" the woman said.

"What for?" the man said.

"I'm working on the case," I said.

He was the slowest study I had ever run into. I counted to five, slowly, and he said:

DEADLINE | 21

"Thought that was pretty well settled."

"He's still alive," I said.

"What is it about Peter?" the woman asked.

Mr. Sampson shifted his feet, hesitated, then stepped out of the way.

"Come on in," he said.

It was a clean, well-kept kitchen. There was white oilcloth on the table. They had been eating from large bowls, and there was a pitcher of milk on the table and a plate with some bread on it.

The woman appeared to be in her middle fifties. Her face had the grooved, deeply indented look of those who work hard for a lifetime and get little from it in the way of material goods. Her hair was gray and straight and cut short. There was evidence that once in a while she put a wave in it, homemade fashion.

"Have you seen Peter?" she asked. "How is he feeling?"

"I haven't seen him," I said, "but I hope to. I don't know how he feels, probably not very good."

"No," she said, "I guess not."

Fred Sampson hovered like a tower at some distance. It was as if, because the woman had shown an interest, he would let me in and let us talk but he wouldn't have anything to do with it himself. Mrs. Sampson offered me a chair and some coffee. I accepted the chair and declined the coffee. Fred Sampson stayed on his feet.

"Peter lived with you people, I understand," I said.

"Yes, since he was twelve years old. He lost his parents, you see."

"And you brought him up."

"Well, I guess you could say that, yes."

"What kind of a boy was he?"

"Oh, he was a good boy! Quiet and well-behaved—and work, my goodness!"

Fred Sampson walked to a shelf, picked out a toothpick, and began to pick his teeth.

"He was a hard worker," he said unexpectedly.

"How did he do in school?" I asked. "Was he a pretty good student?"

Mrs. Sampson looked somewhat embarrassed.

"Well—just average, I guess."

"No good," Fred Sampson said. "He didn't care much for school. Couldn't seem to catch on good."

"But he didn't fail," Mrs. Sampson insisted.

"Kind of a dreamer," Fred said. "Always thinkin' about somethin' else."

I didn't want to take a chance on Mrs. Sampson's getting choked off and drying up on me, so I kept my attention on her.

"Was it a big shock to him, losing his parents?" I asked her. "How did it happen?"

"A young boy like that," she said, "it was very hard. He was the only one. They had a farm down the road here and things didn't go too well for them—it was a poor farm—"

"Davidian was a poor farmer," Fred put in. "Drank. Didn't take to farmin'. You have to take to it."

"He did the best he could, I guess," Mrs. Sampson said, "but things didn't go well at all. And then the fire burned them out—"

"They were killed by the fire?" I asked.

"No, not the fire—accident. Mr. Davidian was driving the car, on the county road—"

"Drunk," Sampson said. "He was drunk."

"Anyway," his wife said, "he hit a culvert, going pretty fast, and it killed both of them, his wife too."

"Peter didn't see it happen?" I asked.

"No, he wasn't with them. He was with us. After the fire, you see, we took Peter in—their house was gone, no money. His parents moved into town and Peter's father did odd jobs around. Then the accident—so we just kind of took care of Peter from then on."

"Glad to do it," Sampson said defensively. "Had none of our own."

"He was such a good boy—so quiet and well-behaved," Mrs. Sampson said.

"The farm that burned," I said, "the Davidian farm—was it the same place where the—where Peter's big trouble happened?"

"You mean where Esther Parrish was killed?" Mrs. Sampson said. "Yes, yes, it was."

I looked up at Sampson.

"You worked that place for a while," I said.

He nodded.

"Couple of years—well, four, five altogether."

"Wasn't a very productive place?"

"Nothing much."

Mrs. Sampson got up quietly and left the table. When she had disappeared from the kitchen, Sampson said: "Took it awful hard, she did, awful hard. Ain't got over it yet. Wakes up in the night sometimes, calling for Peter." I nodded with what I hoped was sympathy.

"Tell me something," I said, "was Peter Davidian a real, normal type of boy?"

He had to do some thinking about that. While he was having his thoughts I had a couple of my own, about the fact that the death of Peter Davidian's parents had brought Fred Sampson an extra farm to work and a boy to help with the chores. "A good worker."

"He was a queer one," Sampson said.

"Can you remember any especially queer things he did?"

"Well—about girls. He was scared of 'em."

"Oh? Not too abnormal in a boy—"

"But Peter—he was real scared. Used to run and hide. They taunted him, picked on him."

"Esther Parrish too?"

He didn't answer right away. Something happened in his face and I couldn't interpret it.

"Esther Parrish was a mighty pretty girl," Fred said. "Never could understand how she could bother somebody like Peter."

"How did she bother him?"

"Oh—tormenting him, way girls do. Teasing—"

"You mean she'd flaunt herself and then back out?"

"I don't know about that. Doubt that Peter would know what to do with a girl. He was too scared."

Either that was as much as he understood about it or he didn't like to discuss it. Mrs. Sampson came back and I stopped pressing the point.

She had a photograph album, one of the old-fashioned kind with black pages and the snapshots pasted in more or less at random.

"He don't want to see those old pictures, Ma," Fred Sampson said.

"I would like to," I said, "if you have time."

Mrs. Sampson had plenty of time, but I had the feeling that Fred wanted to call it off. I remembered that farmers tend to go to bed early.

"This is a picture of Fred and Peter at haying time. Peter was fifteen then."

He was a tall boy at fifteen. Nobody could be as tall as Fred Sampson, but Peter was a lot huskier looking. He had quite a lot of thick, dark-colored hair and a good enough boy's face. The only thing that marred it was that his eyes were badly crossed.

"Did the others tease him much about his eyes?" I asked.

"Oh yes," she said. "You know how children are—pretty mean sometimes. The girls were the worst."

She leafed through the pages slowly. The pictures were typical family snapshots, some clear, some fuzzy. In some Peter was dressed in his Sunday clothes. They didn't fit him too well; he looked ungainly and embarrassed.

"Mr. Sampson was telling me how the girls used to tease him," I said.

She looked up at Fred, as if for permission to speak. I don't know what passed between them.

"Yes, they did. Especially that Esther—"

"Esther Parrish?" I said.

"Now, Ma," Fred said, "all girls do that—"

"Esther Parrish was a slut!" she said.

I looked at her. She had said it with great heat, even defiance, and her face was flushed and mottled with some kind of deep fury.

Sampson kept quiet.

"Did Esther Parrish spend a lot of time out here with Peter? Come out here to see him?" I asked.

"She and that friend of hers, Mary Carpenter—seemed as if they were always out here, one reason and another."

"Well," I said, "did Peter ever have any explanation, I mean for you, why they came out here?"

"Peter never said much," she said quietly. She was still flushed and kept her eyes down now, leafing through the album.

Fred Sampson had no more to say until we had made the complete run of the pictures. Then as Mrs. Sampson closed the book, not without tenderness, he said:

"Close to bedtime."

Without raising his voice, he brought off a firm dismissal. I got on my feet and thanked Mrs. Sampson for showing me the pictures.

"What chance do you think Peter has?" she asked. "Does he have a good lawyer?"

"One of the best," I said. "Sam Birch. We're not giving up."

"It's only, let's see, four more days?" she said.

"A lot can happen in four days," I said. "Not that it will be a sure thing. May I come and see you again?"

"Yes," she said, "any time."

Fred Sampson opened the door for me.

"Thanks," I said. "I'm at the hotel in town, if you think of anything I could use."

"All right, good night," he said.

I went outside and he closed the door firmly behind me.

Not much of a haul, I thought, getting into the car. He was a country boy, worked hard; he was afraid of girls and he didn't talk much. He had the handicap of the strange eyes. In the Big Book he would have lived and died in total obscurity—except that he had for some reason murdered Esther Parrish.

I drove down the country road in the dark and turned into the lane at the abandoned farm where the local boy had made bad with the local girl.

CHAPTER 3

The lane was deeply rutted and at one point I came down off a rock with the sickening lurch that sometimes signifies a broken axle. I pushed the car on to where the ground leveled off in front of the old barn. I hadn't met any traffic in either direction and didn't really expect anyone to be around. Still, I wasn't altogether at home in the country and I didn't want to be surprised in this of all places. I drove across the barnyard, avoiding piles of accumulated debris, and parked the car between the crumbling chimney of the burned-out house and the one remaining wall of an out-building just behind it. The car wouldn't be visible from the road, and by the time I reached the barn door, I had to look hard to spot it myself.

The barn was wide open. The high sliding door had been pushed aside and was hanging from one hinge. There was an odor of decaying wood, dried manure, and rats. I had a flashlight and that portion of my file which included the detailed description of the murder scene, complete with map and pictures. It was very unpleasant material and I had avoided studying it. But it couldn't be put off any longer.

I went in with the light and a large rat came down off a platform near-by and lumbered away. I gave him a little time and got up there myself. With the map in one hand and my flashlight in the other, I got more or less oriented. The platform extended the length of the barn, taking up about a third of its width. It was about eighteen inches above the barn-floor level, which took up two-thirds of the space. Along the platform on the outside were some cattle stalls. In the center of the barn, about eight feet above the platform and between nine and ten feet above the main barn floor, a large tie beam ran from wall to wall. From that tie beam, eight months and a few days before my visit, the nude body of Esther Parrish had been found hanging, head down, dead.

I played the light along the beam. There were no traces left of the "half-inch hemp rope" that had bound her ankles. If it hadn't been cut away at the time, the rats would have done away with it in the course of a few weeks. I played some light on the floor, both levels. There was straw and litter and that was all. There had been a good deal of blood at one time, but it didn't show any more. The rats would have taken care of that too, I decided.

I glanced at some of the photographs the sheriff's department had taken on the scene, but in the surroundings my stomach wasn't up to it. The girl had been badly used. On the day of the crime Peter Davidian had been seen in the company of Esther Parrish and Mary Carpenter, downtown. It was a Saturday and nearly everybody was downtown. The evidence had been firm and convincing. Witnesses had no difficulty remembering that at about four-thirty in the afternoon Peter Davidian had driven into a service station at the east end of town in a pickup truck belonging to Fred Sampson. With him were Mary Carpenter and Esther Parrish. In the truck bed was a wheel and flat tire from Esther's car. It had been brought in to be fixed. Esther had had a flat tire on the county road, and Peter Davidian had come along in the truck and offered to put on the spare. But the spare tire had been flat. So he had brought the tire in to the station, and when it was fixed, he would take it and the girls back to the car and put the good tire on the car so they could drive it.

The three of them had hung around the service station till the tire was fixed, and at about five-fifteen Peter and the girls had driven away in the pickup. Esther Parrish had not been seen alive in town after that. According to Mary Carpenter, they had driven out the county road to where Esther's car was parked, the left rear end jacked up. When Peter started to put the wheel on, something happened to the jack—Mary Carpenter couldn't explain it precisely—and Peter said he'd drive to the farm and get another jack. Esther wanted to go with him, but Mary decided to wait in Esther's car.

She had waited about forty-five minutes and Peter and Esther didn't come back. It was winter and dark by this time and cold, so Mary had flagged down a ride for herself and gone home. Because of mixed feelings of loyalty and resentment at having been left to wait so long, she hadn't said anything to anyone about Esther and Peter until about nine o'clock that night. Then she had tried to call Esther at home. Esther's father, Jack Parrish, had said she wasn't home, he'd thought she was with Mary. So she had told Jack Parrish about the flat tire and the waiting, and the search had begun at that time. At about ten-thirty that night they had found Esther in the abandoned barn, hanging from the tie beam. In one of the cattle stalls they had found Peter Davidian, hiding. He had a knife in his hand and there was blood on the knife. All he had been able to say for himself was that he had discovered Esther there and had been about to cut her down. Then the search party had arrived, he'd got scared and hidden himself in the stall.

It had seemed a lame excuse at the time and it still did. The only explanation he had for the interval between the time they had left Mary on the county road and the discovery of Esther's mutilated body was that after they reached the Sampson farm, where Peter had found the substitute jack, Esther had complained of being too cold to ride back in the truck and said she'd like some coffee. Peter said she could stay in the Sampson house while he went to finish up with the tire. The Sampsons had gone downtown and weren't home. Peter had left Esther in the house and had driven back to the county road. Mary Carpenter had left by that time, and he didn't give it much thought. He jacked up the car and got the wheel on, took Esther's keys out, and drove back to the Sampson farm. Esther wasn't there. He looked through the house and didn't find her and finally decided she was playing another of her jokes on him, according to her custom. So he left the house, replaced the keys in her car on the way into town, and had supper at the Wesley Café. He was seen in there between seven and eight that evening.

The rest of his story was short and no more convincing than the first part. He said he left the restaurant about eight o'clock and hung around town for a couple of hours doing this and that. About ten o'clock he started home to the Sampson place. Peter made no effort to synchronize his movements with those of Fred Sampson and his wife, who were visiting friends.

He was driving past the abandoned farm where he had lived as a boy, when he caught sight of a car parked in the lane, down near the old barn. Out of curiosity he stopped on the road and went back to see who it was. It was Esther Parrish's car and there was nobody in it. He said he walked back to the road, got a flashlight from the truck, and returned to the barn, to investigate. He found Esther hanging from the beam and the knife on the floor of the platform. He picked up the knife—he said he wasn't sure whether she was dead or not—and then he heard the sounds of the search party approaching; he panicked and hid in the stall.

It is the custom in such rural areas for boys and girls to pull off the main road at night for smooching purposes. A deserted barnyard is as good a spot as any. Therefore, one of the weakest parts of Peter's story was that in which he told of seeing Esther's car near the barn and going to investigate. It was weak, that is, unless he had a big case on Esther and was spying on her. But a major element of his testimony and the history I had got from the Sampsons was that he had the opposite of a case on her, that he was afraid of her and that she tormented him. Anyway, the searchers had found no evidence of anyone else's presence on the scene, and after them the sheriff's investigators hadn't found any either. So the prosecution's case had been that Peter had taken all he could from Esther, after going far out of his way to help her with the flat tire and so on, had lost his temper and reason, and had attacked her. He had then driven her to the abandoned barn, where it had come over him to mutilate her. The defense case, based mainly on psychiatric testimony, had been turned against it by other psychiatrists who pointed out that he was retarded sexually and might well act out his suppressed yearnings for her in this murderous way without ever realizing himself that he had any feelings for her except hatred. No psychiatric witnesses on either side, with one exception, had found Peter to be insane, in a legal sense, and the exception wasn't very articulate on the stand and had managed to confuse everyone, including the judge. To make matters worse, evidence had been produced to show that Peter had a violent temper. It was very slow in rousing, but when it hit, it hit hard, blindly, and all-out rough. He had been known to attack a recalcitrant cow with a pitchfork, doing considerable damage before Fred Sampson cooled him down.

Some great client, I thought. And Sam Birch—what did he find himself up against?

But Sam volunteered, I thought. I got drafted.

I wasn't learning anything here, I decided. Not that I'd really expected to. My visit to the barn had been—to strain the vocabulary—a sentimental one.

I looked at a snapshot portrait of Esther Parrish, included in the file as a kind of relief shot among the gruesome studies of her catastrophe. In the uncertain glow of the flashlight I couldn't tell much about her. A pretty girl with a smile. Nice teeth.

I had stuffed the file back into the envelope and was turning to step down from the platform when a car stopped out on the road. A moment later a car door slammed. There wasn't much time for a thought-out decision. Curiosity and, to be honest, a measure of panic drove me across the narrow shelf of the platform, over a waist-high wall into one of the cattle stalls. In the instant before I doused the flashlight I saw that I had landed in a manger. There was some hay in it, moldy and lank, but it was easier to kneel on than plain wood.

Is this the one where Peter Davidian hid that night? I wondered.

Footsteps approached across the barnyard. They didn't pause anywhere, and I decided whoever it was hadn't noticed my car. But I had no idea what that meant, if anything.

A light flashed in the doorway and a man came in behind it. I watched him through a crack in the board at my face. A tall guy, very tall, in overalls. Fred Sampson.

He didn't loiter. He knew where he was going. I watched him cross the lower barn floor toward the corner opposite and beyond where I crouched. Using his light, he bent far over. There were vague rattling sounds, metallic. He straightened and stood for a few seconds, holding the light steady. I couldn't see what he was doing. He bent again; there was more rattling. Then he rose again to his full, extreme height, turned, and walked out of the barn.

I gave him time till the sound of his steps had faded down the lane. I was climbing out of the stall, brushing my pants and jacket free of hay, when the car started up.

In the corner where I had seen him bend and straighten I mined a small mound of old hay with the toe of my shoe. It struck a hard object and I leaned down over it. It was a strongbox, the old-fashioned black, shallow square, rusty here and there where the paint had chipped off. There was a lock, but either it didn't work or he didn't bother with it. When I put my fingers under the flange of the lid, it lifted easily enough. I threw some light into it. There was a thin bundle of currency. Underneath, a couple of smallish paper items. I flipped through the currency without counting it. Mostly it was one-dollar bills. I saw a five.

Fred Sampson's little private cache, I thought. Mrs. Sampson wouldn't know it exists.

I picked up the small stiff rectangle that had lain under the money. A snapshot of a girl. A picture of Esther Parrish. It looked like another print of the one I had examined a few minutes earlier. There was nothing inscribed on it.

The other item was a folded piece of flimsy, the printing showing through. I opened it and the printing came clear. Stenciled in large letters on the face of the receipt were the words: bill of sale. It was from Jack Parrish, Dealer, International Harvester, etc., and under the itemization of one light tractor, with model number and selling price, was written, in longhand, "Paid in full. J. P." The date was seven months earlier.

That would be how he manages to hold out a little cash from the family accounts, I decided. Mrs. Sampson probably thinks he's still paying on the tractor, and he probably pays in cash—or paid.

I replaced things the way I had found them and closed the box, straightened, and kicked some hay over it. It had been a pathetically meager discovery. The snapshot of Esther Parrish bothered me, but that could be meager too.

Suddenly the atmosphere in the crumbling barn was overwhelmingly depressing. I picked up my manila envelope and walked out into the fresh air. Crickets or something were chirping loudly all around me. The night breeze was like a long, cold drink of water after a dusty walk.

Drink, I thought.

I threw the file into the back seat of the car, climbed in and got it started, made my way down the bumpy lane and drove back to town, to the hotel.

* * * *

The lobby was badly lighted and only a little less depressing than the barn. Old Jess was nowhere in sight. Behind the desk was a youngish fellow with a broken-out face and narrow shoulders. On a centrally located divan sat two large fellows. One was the mechanic from Jack Parrish's tractor emporium, Tony Bledsoe. The other was the guy with the cigar whom I had seen briefly in the showroom that afternoon.

At the desk I started to introduce myself to the relief clerk, but he was reaching for my key before I could get the words out. I gathered business hadn't picked up any.

With the key was a message on a slip of paper.

"Call when possible, any time, day or night. Sam Birch."

By the time I had read it, the two from the divan had got up and were leaning on the desk, one on each side of me. I put the slip of paper in my jacket pocket. The one with the cigar shifted it from the left corner of his mouth to the right and spoke my name.

"All right," I said. "And you?"

"Jack Parrish," he said.

I nodded and looked at the other one.

"I think we've met," I said.

His face didn't say anything. It was a roundish, beefy face, with a smashed nose and broken veins here and there. His eyes were funny. They didn't move much, but they didn't look right at me either. I gave up on him and looked at Jack Parrish. His face was in better condition. I noticed that he had very little in the way of a neck, though it was a long way around whatever he had between the head and the shoulders. He was sunburned a little. I couldn't see any resemblance between him and his dead daughter, except maybe a little around the eyes, which, unlike Tony Bledsoe's, were clear and steadily focused.

"Like to talk to you," he said. "How about having a glass of beer?"

The glass of beer part sounded good to me. The manner of the invitation was something else again.

"Where do we go to get it?" I asked. "And how much does it cost?"

"Down the street. I'll buy."

"No," I said. "I'll buy my own."

He shrugged and pushed back from the desk. The pimply one behind the desk was making a great show of unconcern while listening intently with both ears. I could see them twitch.

Tony Bledsoe had moved back with Parrish, as if they were two puppets on one string. It wasn't hard to tell which was in charge.

"I have about twenty minutes," I said.

"Won't take long," Parrish said.

I went out with them and down the hotel steps. It was about nine-thirty now and the street was nearly deserted. There was a light in the Wesley Café and the drugstore was still open. Everything else was closed. I hadn't seen any tavern or such facility in town and I kept wondering whether there was some side street I'd missed altogether.

It turned out that I had missed it and then again I hadn't—I hadn't ever really looked for it. We walked all the way down Main Street past the drugstore and the vacant lot and past the town hall. There were lights on the second floor and the sound of voices came through open windows. A light glowed over the door marked CONSTABLE—JAIL, but there was no light inside. The reason I had missed the side street was that I had not got beyond Roscoe Embers' office in the town hall. There was a paved alleyway running alongside the big square building, and a short block away after we rounded a corner I saw a neon beer sign over a recessed door.

No words had been spoken since we had left the hotel lobby. As he rounded the corner and headed for the sign, Jack Parrish said:

"This way."

It seemed an unnecessary remark. Tony Bledsoe didn't say anything. And that was all right with me.

Three stone steps led down from the lighted door into a basement tavern. Parrish went first, I followed, and Tony Bledsoe brought up the rear. I had gone along with the flanking maneuvers in order to save time and effort. On leaving, however, I would go either first or last, if I had to make a thing of it.

There was a short bar with beer taps. It would accommodate seven and it was filled up. There were some long, family-style tables in the middle of the room and some booths in the back corners. One of them was occupied—by Fred Sampson. The other was vacant. Against the far wall were a jukebox and a cigarette machine. The jukebox, mercifully, wasn't getting any play.

"Take the booth in the back," Parrish said.

Nobody had greeted us. I thought about that for a moment. Parrish would be a big man around town. Either everybody was afraid of him or, because he was with a stranger, everybody figured he was here on business and nobody wanted to nose in.

On the way to the empty booth I caught Fred Sampson's eye and nodded slightly by way of recognition. There was a moment of hesitation and then he seemed to acknowledge me. I couldn't be sure.

I wonder what he tells Mrs. Sampson, I thought, when he takes off like that? "Got to go down to the old barn to pick up a tool." Something like that. According to Roscoe Embers, he had been going down to the old barn to pick up a tool when he discovered the body of Esther Parrish.

Parrish and Bledsoe were waiting for me to slide into the middle of the booth.

"Go ahead," I said.

Bledsoe hesitated, then slid in. I sat down next to him around the corner of the table, and Parrish sat across from me. He raised three fingers high in the air and we sat there in silence while the bartender brought three glasses of beer and set them down.

"Hi, Jack, Tony," he said.

He looked at me uncertainly and half nodded. I nodded in return and put a five-dollar bill on the table. Parrish brought out some money and put it down. Bledsoe just sat there. The bartender went away.

"All right," I said, putting both hands flat on the table. "We got this far. What are we talking about?"

Parrish's cigar danced in four directions. He removed it and drank half the glass of beer at a gulp. It was the first time I'd seen him with the cigar out of his mouth.

"Not too much," he said. "I understand you're looking into the case of Peter Davidian."

"That's right," I said.

"What for?"

I drank some beer.

"A good lawyer," I said, "with a client on death row, keeps working on it up to the last possible minute. Davidian has a good lawyer. I work for him."

Parrish drank the rest of the beer and banged the glass on the table.

"You think you're going to get the kid off?" he said.

"No," I said. "The lawyer is shooting for a commutation."

"What's that?"

The bartender came with two more glasses for Parrish and Bledsoe. Bledsoe hadn't finished his first yet, and the bartender left it. He looked at mine, which I had only sipped from, and went away.

"Instead of the electric chair," I said, "with a commutation, Peter would get life in prison."

"With parole?" Parrish said.

I shrugged.

"Who knows?"

He had another slug of beer, not so big this time.

"Where do you fit in?" Parrish asked. "What's your line?"

"I'm a private detective," I said.

"Chicago?" he said.

I nodded.

No doubt being from Chicago would mean at least three automatic demerits, but I couldn't help it. I lived there.

"How about me asking one?" I said.

He didn't say yes or no, but he waited.

"Are you persuaded in your own mind?" I asked. "You think Peter Davidian ought to get the chair?"

The cigar dipped once, firmly.

"Yeah," he said, "I'm persuaded."

"Then I guess we understand each other," I said. "I realize you sustained a great loss. I sympathize with you. At the same time, I made a commitment to Sam Birch that I'd work on the case till the last minute, along with him, and that's what I'm going to do."

"You have any hopes?" he said.

"I always have hopes."

His eyes shifted and something passed between him and Tony Bledsoe. I couldn't read it.

"Okay," Parrish said. "Just want to say one thing. If Davidian don't sit in that chair, I'll get him. I'll find a way. I damn near got him that night, in that barn, but the sheriff had too many for me. After what Davidian did to my little girl—I'll get him, in or out of jail."

I finished my beer, put my change in my pocket, and got out of the booth.

"That's another matter," I said, "and there's nothing I can do about it. I have no suggestions."

Apparently neither Bledsoe nor Parrish had any further suggestions either. They didn't say anything as I turned away to leave the tavern. I noticed that Fred Sampson had disappeared.

Probably doesn't like to spend time around Parrish, I thought. Hard place to be. Some of it would be bound to rub off on him, even though he was no blood kin to Peter.

Walking back to the hotel, I had to make my way through a small crowd issuing from the meeting on the second floor of the town hall. I didn't see any sign of Miss Caroline Adams, but I didn't linger to search. I stopped at the car, took out my Peter Davidian file, and went into the hotel.

CHAPTER 4

In the lobby, standing at the desk, I talked to Sam Birch. While I was at it, Chris Duval came in from some inner room and began wiping down the furniture with a dust rag. I divided my visual attention between him and the twitching ears of the desk clerk.

"I wish I had more recorded conversation from our boy," I said.

"He's not a talker," Sam said. "Last report I had from Stateville was that he doesn't even bother to say good morning any more."

"You think I'd have any luck if I'd visit him?"

"Anything's worth a try. How is it going? You running into resistance?"

"Well—some."

"Feeling still pretty high, huh?"

"Yeah."

"How about that schoolteacher—Caroline Adams?"

"Nothing yet. Frozen or something."

"You can begin to sense how it would go with a jury, after they saw those pictures."

"Yes, I can sense that."

"So what we're up against—the governor is not a jury, but he's up for re-election. This year."

"Uh-huh."

"And whatever we come up with, Mac, has got to be real strong."

"Uh-huh again."

"Real strong. Okay, give me a ring when you can."

"Good night, Sam."

I hung up and the relief clerk's ears stopped twitching. Chris Duval had worked his way to the far side of the room, and I went over there and sat down where I could look out the window. He was mumbling to himself from time to time, but he wasn't very close and I couldn't make out any words. I wished I had the relief clerk's ears.

Outside an occasional car backed out of a parking slot and drove off down the street. I saw a scattering of pedestrians, heading up Main Street toward the residential section of the town. I assumed they were coming from the school meeting at the town hall.

Chris Duval's dust rag flicked in a corner of my vision. I glanced at him and nodded.

"Hello," I said. "How are you this evening?"

He just ducked his head, dropped his eyes, and worked a little faster. He was mumbling again, though, and that was what I wanted to hear, that mumble-mumble.

Tell me something, Chris, I thought.

"…fourteenth July," he was saying. "Bastille Day. That's my birthday. Bastille Day."

He was great on nativity, including that of chickens.

Duval, I thought. French. His mother told him he was born on Bastille Day and he never forgot.

"What day were you born?" he said.

It was so startling to hear a direct comment from him, I almost turned speechless.

"May," I said. "May fifth."

"What's your name?"

"Mac."

"Mac—May fifth," he said. "I'll remember."

I believe you, I thought. But try to remember something besides whose birthday it is.

"Miss Adams, December twentieth," he said. "Almost Christmas. Her name's Caroline."

"That's right," I said.

"Miss Adams teachin' me to speak French. Never did learn. My folks talked French, never taught me."

"Well—"

"Parley-voo," he said. "That's French."

"Yup."

"Got to go now," he said. "Got to finish up at the drugstore, come back here later."

"Nice talking to you," I said.

He ducked his head and hurried away. I sat there for a few minutes until the sporadic activity outside was obviously in the past, then I got up, hitched my manila envelope up under my arm, and climbed the stairs to my room. Even though I had left the window open, it was stuffy and smelled of old wood and fabric and faintly musty. I left the door ajar, took off my jacket, tie, and shoes, and stretched out on the bed with my hands under my head.

It has sometimes happened for me, though not often, that if I could ease my mind into a state of free-swinging relaxation, not pushing anything, just letting it float like an open boat in a calm sea, I could catch a few unexpected fish. Because there wasn't much else I could do around town late at night, I decided to give it a try. One of the problems was the difficulty of shaking off the bad memory of the death barn, the pitiful figure of Fred Sampson and the photographs of Esther Parrish. They kept darting in like nasty birds, bringing tension. Then once in a while one would fly in from that death cell at Stateville. But that was easier to deal with. It was feeble. It didn't have much life left in it.

After a few minutes I achieved a reasonable state of mind and set myself adrift. Trying to imagine myself being Peter Davidian wasn't easy. My problems with girls at his age had been of a different kind. Also, I had not seen my parents killed at the age of twelve. But I had seen the Sampsons and their farm and the abandoned farm, which his father had worked. I had seen Fred Sampson in various lights and I could feel a little of what it must have felt like to Peter to grow up in that atmosphere. Mrs. Sampson had evidently been kind to him and fond of him. Fred Sampson, very likely, had worked him hard.

Then there were his strange eyes, which would make him a butt of jokes. There were a lot of things going against Peter, and some of them probably would have been bad enough to drive him to go for a stubborn cow with a pitchfork, and so on.

In a court of law, however, to have a history of violent tantrums is not enough to establish irresponsibility. It can indicate a defective personality, but it doesn't indicate legal insanity. As for some of the other well-known "outs," you might kill someone by hitting him—or her—in the head with a club and plead an irresistible impulse, or that you had blacked out momentarily and didn't know what you were doing. But what had been done to Esther Parrish had taken time and some ingenuity, even if fiendish, and it would be awfully hard to sell a jury the idea that Peter didn't know the nature and quality of his act all the way through that time.

My mind turned to Esther Parrish. A pretty girl, no doubt able to pick and choose among boyfriends, her father a big man in town, car of her own—why would she monkey around teasing Peter, spending all that time with him?

One reason could be that she was fairly quirky herself. This led to the fascinating speculation that she was the crazy one, rather than Peter. But it didn't lead very far. There was another possible reason, a better one: she might do it to screen other activities. Say, for instance, she had another boyfriend, a real one, but a forbidden one, like, say, a married man. Esther

Parrish's mother had died when Esther was eight years old, and she had been brought up by her father and various housekeepers. Girls without mothers sometimes get attracted to older men. If such a man happened to live, or if she was in the habit of meeting him, in the vicinity of Peter's home, the Sampson farm, she might use Peter as a cover. It would be mainly a matter of misdirection. People would be distracted by her frivolous, girlish bedevilment with the cross-eyed strange one and wouldn't notice that she was seriously involved with someone else.

Mary Carpenter, I thought, would know whether I was on a scent here. I would have to get acquainted with Mary Carpenter somehow and get her to talk to me.

The act of unmooring my mind and letting it drift, though it had maybe invited some constructive ideas, had also made me sleepy. I was gathering my energy to get up, undress, and get back in bed when brisk footsteps sounded in the hall. I stayed where I was, waiting for her to pass. I wasn't up to playing the game with the door in her face.

She reached the open door of my room looking straight ahead. Then, like nine out of ten people anywhere in the world, she glanced in. Unlike nine out of ten people, instead of snapping her eyes straight ahead again and going on her way, she faltered, hesitated, went past the doorway, stopped, and looked in again.

"Good evening," I said. "How did the meeting go?"

"All right," she said. "I'm sorry, I—"

"Don't give it a thought," I said. "I shouldn't have left the door open."

"Well, I—good night."

"Could I ask you one simple question?" I said.

She waited, hovering, half in flight.

"What?" she said.

"Do you think Peter Davidian was a completely normal American boy, in command of all his faculties?"

She made a gesture of desperation, shook her head, as if to clear it, and went away.

"Good night," she said.

I heard her key in the lock and after a moment the oversharp slam of her door. I looked at the ceiling and saw an image of Peter Davidian, sitting on the bunk in his death cell, just sitting there, waiting.

Somebody talk to me! I thought.

Seldom in my life has a prayer had such an instantaneous response. Her door clicked, opening, and her small heels thudded on the hall carpet. When she looked into the room, her face was tense and white and stormy around the eyes.

"Listen," she said through her teeth, "why don't you go back to—Chicago or wherever you're from—and leave me alone!"

I didn't say anything. There wasn't anything. She backed away, wheeled, and returned to her room, slamming the door, but not quite so hard this time. I got up, closed the door, undressed, and went to bed.

* * * *

Country towns are so quiet in the night you can sometimes hear the neighbors snoring a block away. They get up early, though. When I woke, it was six-fifteen and daylight, but just barely. There were voices on the street, the sound of engines. I remembered that it was Saturday.

I looked out the window and saw people going in and out of the Wesley Café, so I knew that was open. It was a comfort to me.

I put on a robe and slippers, picked up my razor and the towel on the rack on the door, opened the door with extreme caution, and looked both ways. The hall was deserted and the door of the bath stood ajar. So I made that and was dressed and on the street before seven A.M.

In the Wesley Café business was good. Workingmen filled all available spaces at the counter, and two husky waitresses in blue and white uniforms dished up ham, bacon, eggs, bread, and potatoes as if they meant to choke all the horses in the world. I sat down at a table, alone, to wait for my turn. There weren't any newspapers, inside or out, except a copy of the previous day's Chicago *Tribune*. I read in it here and there, but I had read the same things the day before and they didn't have much punch.

Even allowing for the fact that they were busy, it seemed to me I had to wait unnecessarily long to be served. It may have been my imagination, combined with hunger. Eventually they got around to me and I made up for the wait by ordering a big one. When it finally came, it was tasty and it hadn't been poisoned.

At about seven-thirty Jack Parrish came in, sat down at the counter, and ordered a cup of coffee and a piece of apple pie. His presence had a subduing effect on the place. Conversation had been running fairly free and loud, but at Parrish's entrance and while he stayed, it fell off. It was as if everyone were waiting respectfully either to hear him speak or for him to finish and get out. It might have been because of his especially harsh bereavement, though that had happened a long time before. I had an impression there was something else behind it, something like, "The Big Man is here—mind your tongue."

He took no notice of me, and when he was finished with the pie and coffee he tossed some change on the counter and walked out. As soon as the door closed behind him, the rattle and bang of the earlier conversation resumed. Then gradually it faded as, one by one, the early customers finished and went away. By a few minutes after eight I had the place to myself.

That made it a little awkward when Caroline Adams came in and there was nobody to look at but me. She handled herself well, however. Her natural poise seemed to assert itself. She nodded slightly, sat down at a table some distance away, opened a book, and began to read. I couldn't see what the book was, not that it was any of my business.

My business was Peter Davidian and it was time to get down to it, but I was hung up for a fresh start. I would have to talk with Mary Carpenter for sure, but I doubted that I'd get far with her just by knocking on the door and inviting her to a conversation about her murdered friend.

One first step, I decided, since I seemed to be a source of agitation to Miss Adams, was to leave her alone with her breakfast and relieve the pressure. That was easy enough, and I paid my tab, left the Café, and crossed the street to the hotel. Roscoe Embers, the town constable, was coming out as I went up the steps. I said good morning, and he nodded and mumbled something and hurried off down the street. He was wearing a dark-blue uniform, with cap, and even without the gun I had seen hanging in his office, he looked too warm and encumbered for this quiet street.

There were no messages for me. In my room I got out my file and looked at the maps that had been furnished me. I had got to thinking about the night of the murder and that Esther Parrish's car, according to Peter, had been parked in front of the deserted barn, which led him to investigate, he said. Then there were other aspects of the episode of the flat tire and Mary Carpenter's sitting out in the cold, waiting, and after I'd refreshed my mind by reading the detailed summary in the file—for the twelfth time—I decided I needed more eyewitness information. If I couldn't get it from Roscoe Embers, maybe I could get it from the sheriff's office. It was a little more removed from the emotional center of the events.

It meant a drive to the county seat, about sixteen miles away by the county road. It wasn't a fast trip—I had to keep watching for loads of hay and cows crossing the road—but it was pleasant enough and I got to the sheriff's office at nine-twenty.

The Sheriff's Department was housed in an old brick building across the street from a renovated courthouse. There were trees on both sides of the street, and the atmosphere was as bucolic as that of the town of Wesley, but somewhat busier. I had to wait for a shiny black-and-white patrol car to clear the drive before I could turn into the visitors' parking lot.

There hadn't been any renovation of the Sheriff's Department, and inside, the rank, metallic, sweat-laced aroma of law enforcement was the same as I had always known it, from Chicago to New York by way of San Francisco. At a broad, three-sided desk, screened by a brass grille, I faced a gigantic deputy with a face like a brisket of corned beef. I had the names of the officers who had dealt with the case. The principal one was named Peterson. He had arrived early on the scene, had spent several hours interrogating Peter Davidian, and he had done most of the testifying at the trial. I knew of him that he was married, with three children, one in college, that he had the rank of lieutenant in the detective bureau, and that he had been in the service of this county for twenty-two years. The statistics were reassuring.

"If he's around," Brisket-face told me, "Peterson will be on the third floor, end of the hall on your right."

I thanked him and climbed a flight of narrow steps, then another flight, and got to the third floor. At the end of the hall, on a frosted-glass panel, were the words: detective bureau. The "Bureau" would be one small room with half a dozen desks, three windows, two of which were stuck and wouldn't open, one typewriter with a ribbon so worn you'd have to hit the keys with a hammer to get an impression, maybe or maybe not a water cooler, and somewhere an electric fan in need of oil.

Inside, I found I had guessed right except for minor errors. There were only five desks and two windows, neither of which was stuck, which was a good thing because there wasn't any electric fan.

One of the desks was occupied by a youngish deputy in uniform, writing slowly on yellow paper with a dull pencil and the tip of his tongue. An older man in plain clothes sat with his back to me, activating the typewriter with the index fingers of both hands.

"Lieutenant Peterson?" I asked.

The young fellow looked up and stared at me.

"I think he's having a cup of coffee," the one at the typewriter said, without looking around.

The young guy turned in his chair and yelled at a closed door at the back of the room.

"Peterson!"

The door opened and a guy looked out. He was in his late forties, with graying hair and eyes pulled down at the outer corners against the sun. He was in shirt sleeves, his collar open, and he had a paper cup in one hand.

"Yeah?" he said.

It was no place for formal introductions. I crossed the room to the partly open door and showed him my I.D.

"Hello," he said. "What can I do for you?"

"If you have a few minutes," I said, "you could talk to me about the Peter Davidian case."

He looked into his steaming cup.

"Oh," he said. "The one that cut up the Parrish girl."

"Uh-huh," I said.

He seemed to think about it.

"Well—it's kind of closed," he said. "What did you want to know about it?"

"Whatever you can come up with that I don't already know," I said.

He studied the coffee some more.

"What's your interest?" he asked.

"I'm working for Davidian's lawyer, Sam Birch."

"Kind of late, isn't it?" he said.

He looked at me on a level. He had good eyes. I had the feeling that in a controversy I'd rather be with him than against him.

"You know the old saying," I said.

He gave it some more thought, then moved back from the door and pushed it all the way open.

"Okay," he said, "come on in. Cup of coffee? I think there's some left in the pot."

"Thanks," I said.

There was a box of paper cups lying on a scarred table beside a ten-cup electric percolator. I dug one out and held it under the tap. There was at least enough in the pot to fill my cup.

"They trying to make out the kid is too crazy, huh?" he said. "Shouldn't be executed?"

"Something like that," I said.

"He wasn't crazy," Peterson said. "I talked to him quite a lot. He wasn't any more crazy than you or me."

"All right," I said. "About the girl, Esther Parrish. Did you have any personal acquaintance with her—alive?"

"No," he said. "I knew her father a little. Not too well."

"Or the other girl, Mary Carpenter?"

"Huh-uh. She didn't figure much in it."

"I know, but she was in it some, and she was a friend of Esther Parrish's, and on the day of the crime she was around quite a lot when Peter Davidian was trying to change the tire—"

He gestured impatiently.

"All that was before—in the afternoon."

"That's true. But a thing keeps bothering me. Esther and Peter drove off to the Sampson farm to get a jack and left Mary sitting in the car. It was cold. Mary got tired of waiting and hitchhiked into town."

He waited.

"She didn't hang around long," I said. "And it must have been warmer in the car than out on that road."

"So?" Peterson said.

"Mary's explanation—official explanation—was that she got cold and tired of waiting and just lit out. But suppose there was another reason?"

"What other reason?"

"One possibility—it was a setup, between Mary and Esther Parrish. On the theory, for instance, that Esther had a rendezvous and used both Peter and Mary Carpenter to help her make it."

He stared at me for a few seconds.

"That's one possibility," he said.

His tone was sarcastically patient.

"Other possibility," I said, "which could be tied all the way into the first one—Mary Carpenter ran for home because she was scared."

His eyes changed and he was listening now.

"Scared of what?" he said.

"That Peter was about to flip, and she sensed it."

He did something with the muscles of his jaw, slowly crumpled his empty cup in his hand, and tossed it into a wastebasket.

"That's a good try," he said. "Seems to me Mr. Birch tried it too. But it don't work."

"I'm listening," I said.

"In the first place," he said, "there never was any evidence that Esther Parrish was fooling around with anybody, not even Davidian. In the second place, if he was about to flip, and if it was noticeable to Mary Carpenter, it must have been noticeable to other people, too, and lots of other people saw him that very day and nobody said anything about him being crazy. In the third place, if Mary Carpenter was that scared, she would have been scared for her friend, Esther, and she would have tried to get help, or she would have told somebody about it. But she didn't do a damn thing about it till nine o'clock that night."

He made a lot of good common sense and I admired it. I didn't stay with my theme, not because he had demolished it, but because all I wanted at the moment was to plant the idea. I could see now that the idea had been planted before, but it couldn't do any real harm to fertilize it a little.

"Would you tell me something about Davidian at the time he was apprehended?" I said. "What seemed to be his state of mind?"

He looked at a watch on his wrist and made a face as if sighing. I gathered he had been over this ground many times.

"I appreciate the time you're giving me," I said. "I wouldn't push it except time for Peter Davidian is getting even shorter."

He nodded and massaged his face with both hands.

"First," he said, "he was scared. They found him in that stall in the old barn. Time I got there, Jack Parrish was there, and I guess he's what Davidian was really scared about. He had a right to be. Parrish would have killed him. Took three of us to cool Parrish off, keep 'em apart.

"So—he had this knife in his hand—Davidian did—and there was blood on it, and there was blood on his clothes and it didn't look good at all. It never did look any better."

"When you interrogated him," I asked, "what was it like? Did he say anything at all, on his own, I mean?"

"Damn little. What could he say? Mostly he said, 'What happened? I don't know what happened.' I kept telling him what happened, but he didn't seem to connect it up. We didn't push him around any. He would sit there with those funny eyes—I guess he was looking at the end of his nose."

"He didn't break down any? Did he express any regret or remorse?"

"Not that I remember. After about five hours he put together a story for us—it's all in the record—"

"I've got that," I said.

"Then I guess you've got about all there is. He wasn't a talker. What he did say, most of it you couldn't believe it. But he wasn't crazy, that I know."

"He kept saying, 'What happened? I don't know what happened.'"

"Well, he might have blacked out, while he was doing it or after—but that's not the same as crazy, any witness will tell you that."

"I know it. All right. The main thing is you were satisfied that he was more or less in his right mind, responsible."

"He sure as hell was."

I thanked him for his time and turned to go.

"On top of which," he said, "he confessed."

I looked over my shoulder.

"He confessed?" I said.

"Sure. Isn't that in your record?"

"No."

"It didn't get into the trial testimony. But then, that trial got pretty fuzzed up before it was over."

"You say he confessed. He said to you in so many words, 'I killed her—I killed Esther Parrish'?"

"Not those exact words, but close enough. I remember it pretty good. He said, 'I guess I did it—I guess I did it. She made me goofy. I went goofy.'"

I believed him when he said he remembered it.

"He said she made him goofy. Did he ever explain what he meant? What she did, if anything?"

"No. Who knows? What difference does it make? Even if she teased him—whatever she did—you don't kill a girl."

"Yes," I said, "that's right. You don't kill a girl for teasing."

I thanked him again and walked through the squad room, down the narrow stairs, and out into the fresh air. There was a drugstore on the farther corner and I walked over there, ordered a cup of coffee at the soda fountain, and went into the telephone booth. I put in a call to Sam Birch and he was out. I said I'd wait for him to call back and returned to my coffee. It wasn't very good coffee, which was surprising to me. You're always supposed to get delicious coffee in the country.

Or, I decided, there was something affecting my taste buds, something, say, like the impossibility of the case of Peter Davidian.

Mary Carpenter, I kept thinking, knows more than she has ever told.

But that could be wishful thinking.

And how much does Caroline Adams, the schoolteacher, know that she hasn't told?

Probably not much specific, I thought. But she might be able to do some shrewd guessing—which wouldn't have helped anybody during the trial, but which maybe now—

I went to the phone again and called the Clark Hotel in Wesley. Old snow-head Jess came on and I asked to speak to Miss Adams.

"No phones in the rooms," he said.

"I know. I thought if she's in, you could maybe send someone up—"

"Nobody here right now. Have her call you if she comes in."

"Never mind, I'll call later," I said.

"Do that," Jess said.

I ordered another cup of coffee, and either it was better than the one before or I was getting used to it. I began to be impatient with Sam Birch for not calling back. I couldn't sit here all day long. Every time I glanced at a clock something spasmodic happened in my stomach.

Cut it out with the self-pity, I told myself. There's a clock running for Peter Davidian too.

It all depends on what you're waiting for, I decided. Sam called back at about eleven-fifteen.

"Sorry to keep you waiting," he said. "I'm in court and we just got a short recess."

"Okay," I said. "I talked to the guy in the Sheriff's Department. Lieutenant Peterson. He said Davidian confessed."

"Yeah—well—a confession, Mac, is something a guy says after they've been on him for hours, so they'll leave him alone."

"I understand that, but—"

"Besides, there wasn't any issue with us whether or not Davidian did it. The issue was his sanity."

"He told Peterson she made him 'goofy.'"

"Yes."

"Did he ever tell you exactly how she made him feel goofy? I mean, was it like a fellow might say, she got him stirred up and anxious, or did he mean he went all the way out, got lost?"

"He never could tell us specifically much of anything. That's what made it tough."

"But he told you enough to persuade this psycho group that he was off balance?"

"They think he can be shown to have been mentally and emotionally irresponsible."

"Yeah," I said. "The feeling around here is different."

"I know it is. Look, can I help you by talking to Davidian? I can get down there to see him late in the day."

"Ask him to talk—just for God's sake to talk. Ask him about Mary Carpenter."

"Mary Carpenter—all right."

"And try to get him to say how he really felt about Esther Parrish—when he didn't have a knife in his hand—and whether she made him any promises she had no intention of keeping."

"Okay..."

"And that's enough for now. If I can get a handle on anything, I'll go talk to him myself, maybe tomorrow."

"Anything you want from any of the doctors, psychologists?"

"I'll take any kind of help I can get."

"I'll talk to them. Hang in, Mac."

"You know me," I said.

I hung up, paid for my coffee, and walked back to the Sheriff's Department where I had parked my car. As I opened the door, Lieutenant Peterson came out by a rear door in the building. But he was on the run and so was the guy with him, and I didn't interrupt them.

CHAPTER 5

You can't operate in a country town the way you do in the city. Mary Carpenter lived in a three-story frame house on a wide, tree-lined street, half a dozen blocks away from the business section. Each house on the block was different from the others; each had a large lawn around it, and there were no cars but mine parked on the street. Without being too alarmed about Roscoe Embers, the constable, I could see that for me to hang around there in broad daylight, waiting to pounce on a young lady right in front of her own house, would show bad judgment.

I drove downtown to the hotel and used Jess's desk telephone to call Sam Birch again. This time he came on right away.

"Another thing to ask the kid when you talk to him," I said. "About Fred Sampson. Try to get an idea of how he felt about Sampson, how he was treated, how hard he had to work."

"He worked hard, I can tell you that. The one thing he would talk about was how hard he worked on that farm."

"Was he mistreated?"

"Maybe—somewhat. That's not so clear. Peter was pretty husky, though. I doubt that Sampson actually pushed him around physically."

"He never said much about how he really felt about Sampson?"

"He didn't like him, but it was hard for him to talk about it. Sampson had made him feel obligated—orphan boy and all that."

"I see. Well, if you can get him to talk about Sampson—"

"I will. Anything else?"

"Maybe later," I said.

As I hung up the phone, Caroline Adams came from the stairs and crossed the lobby, heading out. I went out behind her. On the front steps I said:

"Miss Adams—please—"

She was one step from the sidewalk when I spoke and she lost her balance momentarily and had to perform a little jump in order to complete the descent. My luck was running incredibly bad. I hadn't wanted to put her at a disadvantage.

She took a few seconds to regain some composure, then looked around and up at me. That was bad, too, and I hurried to get down on the same level with her, approximately. I had several inches on her in height, but there wasn't anything abnormal in that.

"Yes?" she said.

"I need help," I said.

"I've told you, I think," she said, "that I—"

"That is right," I said. "But you may be able to help me in ways you haven't thought of."

"What ways?" she asked, bristling.

"Legitimate ways," I said, "out in the open, perfectly healthy—"

"What are you suggesting?"

"I'm trying to get around to suggesting we have lunch together. I will be glad to take you to lunch or to make it on any terms you like."

The corners of her mouth made suppressed feminine gestures.

"The Wesley Café?" she said.

"Preferably not," I said, "but I don't know the area—"

"I can't let you take me to lunch."

"We could go dutch."

"Promise?"

"I promise."

"There is a place out on the highway—nothing really fancy, but it's quiet usually and adequate—"

"Just tell me which turns to make."

She opened her mouth and closed it. She had quite a pretty mouth and it was pleasant to watch it move.

"I think I'd better meet you there," she said. "You just go west on Main Street, about five miles, turn right and go about a mile. It's called the Glade."

"I'll see you there."

"All right," she said.

She walked away with that brisk, trim stride. Her summer skirt whipped smartly at the backs of her knees.

They talk about her, I thought. I wonder what they say?

* * * *

The Glade was a low-roofed, rambling structure with a coffee-shop kind of restaurant at one end, a tavern at the other, and a general store in between. Outside were a couple of gas pumps. Miss Adams was getting out of her car, a modest three-year-old economy model, when I pulled in.

"Would you enjoy a drink before lunch?" I asked her.

She looked carefully in all directions.

"Yes, I'd enjoy it," she said, "but I'm not sure it would be wise."

"I won't ply you with it," I said. "You lead, I follow."

She gave it about twenty seconds' thought, turned away, and went to the door under the sign that read "Cocktails."

Inside it was dimly lighted and fairly cool. There were some booths and along one wall, with windows, some small tables for two. Miss Adams went to one of the tables.

There was nobody else in the place except the bartender, who hadn't got his white jacket on yet and who took our order in his shirt sleeves. If he recognized Caroline Adams, he gave no sign of it.

"I practically never drink before lunch," she said.

"If you'd rather not—" I said.

"No, I rather would. School starts next week. I might as well have my little fling for the season."

The drinks came and they were good enough.

"You've been teaching in Wesley for three years?" I said.

"Longer, actually," she said. "I've been at the high school for three years. I taught two years in the junior high school in town. The high school is a consolidated county school."

"Do they treat you all right?"

"Quite well. You have to start somewhere—this is where I started."

"Where did you study?"

"Northwestern."

"Well, what do you know?—we're both North Siders."

"How far north are you?" she said.

"Nothing as fancy as Evanston," I said. "Near north right now. I was born farther out, in the slums."

"I've always wondered how it feels to be born in a city like Chicago."

"It feels—I don't know how it feels to be born. Living around Chicago in my early youth I keep trying to forget. It didn't feel good."

"I was born in a town like Wesley, a little smaller."

"How does that feel?"

She laughed a little in a friendly way.

"As with you," she said, "all I remember was growing up. It wasn't bad in my case. I was lucky."

I couldn't tell about her. There was an appearance of loosening up, of some rapport between us. But she lived with a taut reserve and I was afraid to push her too hard.

"Are you some sort of policeman?" she asked, not quite looking at me.

"I'm a private detective. I do odd jobs—collect a few bills, trace a few missing persons, that sort of thing."

"And try to release condemned murderers from prison?"

It was an intense and leading question. Some of her intensity showed in her face. I managed to smile.

"Suppose we put it another way?" I said. "How about—investigate the circumstances surrounding a homicide?"

She shrugged.

"Is homicide cleaner than murder?"

I could see that we were only arguing and tried to change the subject.

"Do you live permanently at the hotel, during the school term?" I asked.

"Of course not," she said. "I have a room in a private home, like all proper schoolmarms. But this fall my room wasn't ready when I came, so for a few days I'm staying at the hotel."

"Do you like living in a private home?"

"Well—yes and no. The one I'm living in now is quite grand, and it's well-kept and quiet at night. And of course it's much more reasonable than the hotel."

"Uh-huh."

"I'd have to pay at least seventy-five dollars a month at the hotel, and no private bath. For the room I only pay thirty dollars. The Carpenters don't need the money especially."

"The Carpenters," I said.

"Yes—I've lived there for two years."

"Does Mary Carpenter live there too?"

"Yes. Mary is in one of my classes."

"I see. Are you hungry? Shall we order some lunch?"

"I'm starved."

We found we could have lunch in the tavern and decided to stay there. Miss Adams ordered a ham-and-cheese sandwich on rye and a glass of iced tea. I ordered the same, on whole wheat, and coffee. She declined a second drink and I didn't have one either.

"What about this fellow Chris Duval?" I asked. "He said you're teaching him French."

"Oh, that's one of Chris's jokes," she said. "He asks me if I'll teach him French and I say whenever he's ready to start. Then he says, 'Parley-voo—that's French,' and I agree with him. He never really gets around to signing up for the course."

"He has quite a memory, especially for birthdays."

"He remembers everything. Right now he's on a birthday kick. He's one of those rare types—all he knows is what he remembers. He can't do anything with it except to repeat it, but he remembers."

"How do you know when he's talking to you and when he's just talking to himself?"

"You can't always tell. But usually, if he talks so you can hear it, he means for you to listen."

"How does he get along here? Does he live alone? How do they treat him?"

"He lives alone in a little house at the east edge of town. The children torment him sometimes, but he takes it pretty well. Once he hit a boy in the face with a wet mop, but nothing came of it. He's quite stolid and patient most of the time."

The door opened and a middle-aged couple came in, followed by a husky man of about the same age. The man was Jack Parrish. The couple went to a booth across the room, and Parrish sat down at the bar with his back to us. He was wearing a blue denim shirt and light-tan work pants. The bartender drew him a glass of beer and went to take the order in the booth. Miss Adams took a dainty bite of her sandwich and studied her plate.

"Have you met Mr. Parrish?" she asked.

"Yes," I said.

She put the remains of the sandwich on her plate, wiped her fingers carefully, and pressed her middle fingers against her temples.

"I have gone out with Mr. Parrish on two or three occasions," she said. "Out of courtesy I ought to speak to him, even ask him to join us."

I shrugged.

"You are in charge," I said.

Her voice dropped a few decibels.

"However," she said. "I do not want to be left with Mr. Parrish."

"All right."

She looked around and somehow, in a way mysterious to me, caught Parrish's eye in the bar mirror. I guess it wasn't really mysterious. He hadn't taken his eyes off her since he had entered the room.

"Hello, Jack," Caroline Adams said. "Will you join us?"

He hesitated, looked into his beer, then scooped the glass up in a big hand, left the bar, and came to the table. There was an extra chair and I pushed it out for him. He nodded to me, said, "Hello, Caroline," and sat down.

He was bigger than I remembered. He had this thick neck, sunburned a deep red, and his face was square and broad, with a solid, thrusting chin.

He was wearing a high-peaked cap and he didn't bother to take it off for Miss Adams.

"I believe you've met," she said, waving toward me.

"Yeah," Parrish said. "How are you?"

"Fine," I said. "And you?"

"Okay."

It was hard to tell from his manner what he had going for Caroline Adams. The chances were good that he had quite a lot going. She was young, attractive, spirited, and he was a single man not getting any younger and a big enough man around town to feel sure of himself. He could have a big thing going for her. In which case he wouldn't like it much that I had got her out here tête-à-tête.

"Still working on your—research?" Parrish asked.

"Still working on it. Took a little time out for lunch."

Caroline Adams' brows twitched in what I took to be gratitude. Something else he could have going, I thought, would be that he doesn't like me going around asking questions about his murdered daughter. Caroline Adams would probably know quite a lot about his reactions to it, and naturally she had known Esther rather well. I felt like Agent Zero Zero Seven among the Destroyers.

"More iced tea?" I asked Miss Adams.

She shook her head.

"No, thanks," she said. "I've had just enough of everything."

If the remark had a double edge, Parrish gave no sign that he took it that way. He drank down his beer and looked around for service.

"May I buy you a drink?" I asked.

"No," he said.

Well, I thought, we understand each other to that extent.

"I really must go now," Caroline Adams said, rising.

The bartender appeared.

"Another beer, Mr. Parrish?" he said.

Parrish got to his feet.

"Never mind," he said. "Got to go."

I got on my own feet and asked for a check. Miss Adams was frowning slightly. She had worked herself into an awkward place and she was too polite by nature to just say goodbye firmly and walk away, thus shaking both of us. She vacillated long enough for me to get my check and pay it, and then she left the table and headed out. I followed and Parrish came along at my shoulder.

We jammed up at the door because Miss Adams suddenly remembered that we had made an agreement.

"I almost forgot—I didn't pay for my share of lunch," she said.

Parrish hung around like an eager vulture while she opened her purse, dug into it, and found some bills and change.

"How much was it?" she said.

I was thinking, Oh goddam it, but I managed to say, "One dollar and fifty-five cents."

"Plus tip," she said.

"Twenty cents tip. One seventy-five."

She counted out the exact change, extracted a dollar bill from a loose, slim wad, and put the money in my hand. Parrish watched without expression.

"All right," I said, "we're square."

"Good, and thanks," she said.

She turned quickly, pushed the wrong side of the door, reached for the other side, and Jack Parrish's large right hand beat her to it. The door swung wide and she stepped outside.

"After you, please," I said to Parrish.

He went out and I followed. I had to move quite a distance around him to get to Miss Adams' car door by the time she did. She unlocked it and I opened it for her and waited while she slid in under the wheel.

"We'll do it again soon, I hope," I said.

"Yes," she said, hurrying to get the key in the ignition.

"Will you help me get together with Mary Carpenter?"

"Get together how?" she said.

The car started with a roar and Parrish strolled toward us. His pickup truck was parked next to Miss Adams' car on the other side from mine.

"I need very much to talk to her," I said.

"I don't know—"

"I'll see you about it at the hotel," I said.

"All right."

I moved back, closed the door, and waited while she backed out, turned, and straightened out onto the road. Parrish was leaning against the side of his truck, watching her go.

"Well," I said, "see you later maybe."

He let me take a couple of steps. Then he said, "Listen—"

I stopped and looked around, not turning much.

"What?" I said.

"If you were smart," he said, "you'd go back where you came from."

"Before long," I said. "Anyway within a week."

"Can't make it sooner?"

"No."

He pushed heavily away from the truck and came to me, stabbing with his right thumb over his shoulder in the direction in which Miss Adams had gone.

"That girl belongs to me," he said.

"In fee simple?" I said.

"Never mind. Just keep clear of her—and me."

His voice gave him away. He was a lot more upset than he wanted to show. I had that sudden sense of instant fight in him. But I didn't really want to and I certainly didn't have time. I found something to look at just over his left shoulder.

"You know," I said, "when it gets a little cooler, we could go a few rounds just for the hell of it. But it's pretty hot today and I've got a lot to do. I don't know when the weather begins to moderate here and I may have to leave before that. I will be glad to give you my address and telephone number and arrange a meeting. Until then, I guess you'll just have to excuse me."

He didn't say anything, but I hadn't expected him to say anything, so that was all right. I walked away to my car and got in it, and he was still standing there, brooding or something, when I pulled away.

On the way back to the hotel I stopped at the town hall. Roscoe Embers, the constable, was shuffling papers around with his tiny pale hands. When he looked up at me his eyes, twitched once, then went opaque like the eyes of a sleeping dog.

"I'm looking into the murder of Esther Parrish," I said. "You may remember—"

His head bobbed brusquely.

"Remember. What about it?"

"I just had a talk with Lieutenant Peterson over at the courthouse."

"Yup. I know."

"Then maybe you know what we talked about."

He shrugged and moved the little hands.

"About the case, I guess."

"What I was trying to learn from the lieutenant was whether Esther Parrish might have teased Peter Davidian till he couldn't take it any longer. Can you tell me anything about that? What kind of a girl was Esther Parrish?"

His eyes flicked again in that nervous way and he shook his head for no particular reason.

"She was just an ordinary small-town girl about seventeen years old, nice-looking girl, friendly."

He leaned heavily on the desk and one of his small hands made a stab at the air in front of me.

"Now let me give you some advice," he said. "Don't go around this town asking questions like that about Esther Parrish and all that. You only storing up trouble for yourself and everybody."

I blinked.

"For myself—I can understand that," I said. "But whom else could I make trouble for? What kind of trouble?"

The little hand showed exasperation.

"I don't mean that kind of trouble—kind you're thinking about. I just mean—that case is closed. Everybody decided, way up to the Supreme Court. The girl is dead. Peter Davidian did it. He even admitted it. You keep stirring things up, folks will get down on you."

"Well, I have to run that risk," I said. "I've got a job here. I get paid for it."

He shook his head sadly.

"No use," he said. "Nothing to find out. Just forget it." It came to me then that what he meant by "trouble" was trouble for him, for anybody who talked to me about the case. Trouble from Jack Parrish. I'd seen the trouble start to work for Caroline Adams—nothing violent, but the thing was there working under the surface. Jack Parrish with his red neck and big hands was the local power. Everybody in town could see it symbolized every day in the heavy equipment in his showroom and garage. And all the paper he surely held, financing, was no symbol but real, solid power.

As I left the constable's office, Parrish drove by on Main Street, somewhat recklessly, leaning on his horn. A dog crossing the street stopped in confusion, turned one way, then the other, and managed to escape being run down.

I got in the car and headed for the hotel.

Parrish, I was thinking, we may have to have that meeting earlier than I thought.

In a way it was understandable. He had been cheated out of dealing with Peter Davidian in his own way. Next best was the state's way, and Parrish would see to it that nobody got cheated again. It had become, I decided, a matter of honor with him.

CHAPTER 6

Caroline Adams was trying to open the screen door of the hotel with her foot when I went up the stairs. I opened it for her. She had a heavy box in her arms and her none-too-broad shoulders were drawn down pitifully. "Let me take it," I said.

She hesitated, then gave in.

"Thanks," she said. "It's full of books."

"It sure is," I said, taking it from her. "This is moving day?"

"Just partly," she said, going ahead of me to open her car.

I set the box on the floor of the back seat.

"You have more of these?" I asked.

"Two more."

"I'll get them down for you."

"I'm sure you have other things—"

"I have. But what I do about them pretty much depends on you."

"I don't know what I can do for you."

"Let's get those boxes in the car and that will give you a little time to think about it."

"Well…"

We went across the lobby and upstairs and she pushed open the door to her room. Everything was orderly except for the two boxes, filled with books and papers, sitting on the floor near the bed.

"My room isn't quite ready," she said, "but Mrs. Carpenter said I could bring the books over and put them away. It will help when I really move in."

"Sure."

I carried one box down to the car and when I got back for the other, she had her purse on her arm, ready for the street.

"How about at the other end?" I said.

"Oh, I'll manage—"

"Better let me go along and tote them in. Is that the word, 'tote'?"

"Good a word as any."

"Is Mary Carpenter likely to be at home?"

She didn't answer till we had got outside and I was putting the third box into the back seat.

"I don't know," she said. "It's rather likely."

"It's urgent that I talk with her."

"About the—case?"

"Yes."

She didn't like being pushed and I couldn't blame her for that, but the time had come to do some pushing. More was involved than whim or fancy.

She set her white teeth down on her lower lip for a moment, looked off across the street, then shrugged.

"All right," she said, "I'll accept your help. If Mary is there, I'll introduce you."

"I will appreciate it very much."

"If you'd rather have your own car..." she said. "I'll be there for a while, sorting things."

"It's a short walk," I said, "if you don't mind."

"No, I don't mind."

We got in the car then; she backed away from the curb and drove carefully down the street, past the town hall, turned up the alley that led to the next street, and turned again. Within two minutes we were approaching the high old Carpenter house that sat back among high old trees. Caroline Adams turned into a broad driveway which made a slow, looping turn past the garage and alongside the house. There was a front porch and a wide front door, but Miss Adams stopped at a side door toward the rear. It was by way of a service porch, screened on three sides. A buxom woman of forty-five, wearing a white dress, looked out. Caroline Adams waved.

The woman came out to meet us as we left the car. She moved ponderously, as if her feet hurt. Her face was fat and dimpled, and there was a beading of moisture on her upper lip. The weather would be hard on her.

"Hello, dear," she said to Caroline Adams.

"Mrs. Carpenter," Miss Adams said, "this is Mr.—"

I spoke my name and she repeated it.

"He very kindly offered to help me with these boxes."

"How do you do, I'm sure," Mrs. Carpenter said.

I opened the back door and lifted one of the boxes. Caroline Adams and Mrs. Carpenter were talking, but they weren't saying anything about Mary.

"I'm sure it will be ready for you on Monday," Mrs. Carpenter said. "Will that be soon enough?"

"Just fine," Caroline Adams said. "Thanks so much for letting me bring the books over."

"Well, if you have to leave everything till the last minute..." Mrs. Carpenter said vaguely. "This way."

She opened a screen door and stood back, and I followed Caroline Adams into the house. The entrance was into a large, formal dining room. Across the room, beyond a long table spread with a linen cloth, a flight of stairs rose to a landing. Miss Adams went in that direction and I followed. Mrs. Carpenter stopped just inside the room and waved a fat hand.

"Just anywhere, dear," she called. "They won't be in anybody's way."

"Thank you," Miss Adams said.

She didn't waste any time getting up the stairs. At the landing they made a right-angle turn and went up steeply to a second floor. A hall ran the width of the house and rooms opened from it on both sides. There was evidence that painters were working around the place. A stepladder leaned against the wall beside an open door and there was a folded dropcloth. Miss Adams was heading along the hall toward an open room at the far west end. There was a strong smell of fresh paint.

Bright sunlight flooded the room through high windows from which shades and curtains had been removed. A four-poster bed was covered with a dropcloth. A desk and three chairs had been pushed into the middle of the room to clear the walls for the painters. In one corner a door stood open on a roomy wardrobe and storage closet. It appeared to be empty.

"I guess over there in the closet," Miss Adams said, pointing.

I went to the open door and leaned in with the box. The closet wasn't empty. A feminine voice said: "Boo!"

I dropped the box. A corner of it landed on my left foot. The voice let out a startled yip. The switch from the bright sunlight to the half-dark closet had blinded me and I couldn't see anything.

I gave the box a push to get it off my foot and straightened up, backing out into the room.

"Mary...?" Miss Adams said.

I glanced at her and she seemed to be in some distress. I backed farther away, wishing I could take my shoe off and rub my foot.

A girl appeared in the open doorway of the closet. She was wearing blue jeans and a sweat shirt with the sleeves cut off just above the elbow. On the front of the shirt was a picture of Mozart. She wore no shoes. Like her mother, she was heavy-set, with a round face and wispy brown hair in a random series of straight strands. She wore large spectacles with heavy black rims. She had pimples. She was possibly the least attractive teen-age girl I had ever seen in my life. Aside from her appearance, the little business of hiding in the closet in order to say "Boo" gave me a dim view of her mental powers, if any. I found myself thinking, "Peter Davidian, you are dead."

"Mary," Miss Adams said, "you shouldn't startle people that way when they're carrying something."

Mary put her left forefinger in her mouth. I really couldn't tell whether it was the real thing or a put-on.

"This is Mr.—"

I repeated my name for her again.

"Mary Carpenter," Miss Adams said.

"Hello, Mary," I said.

The girl looked at Miss Adams, as if for support, then at me and then at the floor.

"Hi," she said.

"I'll go down and get the other boxes," I said and fled the room.

When I got back with the second box, Miss Adams and Mary Carpenter were nowhere to be seen. I took half a minute to catch my breath and made another trip downstairs and back with the box, the heavy one. Miss Adams was waiting for me this time, alone.

"I'm sorry," she said, as I stowed the box in the closet.

"No harm done," I said. "Is she all right?"

Miss Adams didn't care for the question.

"I don't know what you mean by all right," she said.

"I mean in general, in most ways?"

"Yes, she's all right. She's sometimes a little childish."

"Mmn," I said.

"She's in her own room. I told her you were interested in the Esther Parrish case and wanted to talk to her and she—just ran away."

I now had small hope that, even if she should listen to some questions, she would be able to give me any useful answers.

"Maybe some other time," I said.

I headed out and she let me get through the bedroom doorway into the hall. The she came after me.

"Wait," she said.

I waited.

"Come in," she said, standing back in the doorway.

I went back in and she pushed the door to, not quite putting it on the latch. She turned from me, walked to the bed, and sat down. When she said something it came over her shoulder and I saw her in profile.

"She's a—not a dull girl—I mean Mary," she said. "But she needs help, certain kinds of help. No need to go into all the reasons—I'm not sure I could even explain most of them. Anyway, that's the reason I live here instead of somewhere else. I've an arrangement with the Carpenters. It works out because she goes to school to me and we can spend extra time together—but that's beside the point."

"All right," I said. "I'm listening. You've been protecting her from things—things like me, for instance. I accept that. But—"

"All right. Yes, I thought I was protecting her. But now I'm not sure. Things aren't all that simple. There's Peter Davidian too. And you have a right to do your job."

"I don't know whether I have a right to. I've signed up to do it, that's about the extent of it. One way or another—"

"I know. Listen—Mary had a very intense relationship with Esther Parrish. They were close, like two parts of the same mechanism. I don't know why it was like that for Esther. I didn't know her very well. But for Mary it was her whole way of life. So when Esther was—killed—it hit Mary very hard. She still hasn't got over it. She's just floating around."

"Good so far," I said. "I'm with you."

"This isn't an uncommon thing, this devotion of friendship, among kids. Boys go through it too."

"Sure."

"In this case, though, it was kind of—unnatural. Not sexually, that I know of, but otherwise, psychologically—the main reason being Esther Parrish. It was a very paradoxical thing, I'm trying to say—the relationship itself was important to Mary, but Esther Parrish was about the worst possible person she could have picked."

I let a couple of suitable moments go by.

"Why?" I said.

"Because…" She moved suddenly on the bed and pushed with both hands, as if to push the conversation away. "Oh, damn it," she said, "I didn't want to get into all this. Why don't you just talk to her and find out for yourself?"

"Whatever you say."

"No—wait. Will you be gentle with her? Take it easy?"

"Easy as possible. I'm not a brutal guy."

"Yes, I know. I believe you. But the material is rough, very rough."

"It is indeed."

"Esther Parrish was a wild one. Very pretty. Sexy. And restless. I used to think that the reason she put up with Mary was because she knew she had to be under some kind of control and she couldn't manage it herself. She didn't get much help from her father."

"What happened to her mother?"

"She died—twelve, thirteen years ago. Jack—Mr. Parrish—brought Esther up with the aid of various housekeepers. They were all good enough women, I guess, but they weren't Esther's mother."

"How wild was she? She ever get into real trouble, man trouble?"

"Not that I know of, but she was always on the edge of it."

"Boys?"

"Uh—no, more like older men. Older for her."

"Could you mention a few names?"

"No. Not that I really know of."

"I'd accept mere suspicion at this point."

"I can't do that."

"All right. Do you suppose Mary could?"

She squeezed her shoulders forward, as if trying to make them meet.

"I don't know."

"Will it get too distressing for her if I push it a little?"

"Everything gets distressing to her, almost right away." I thought about it briefly.

"You don't leave me much hope," I said.

"I'm just trying to give you the background."

"I know and I appreciate it."

"You will take it easy with her?"

"I don't see that I have any choice. Yes, I'll take it easy."

She got up and opened the door.

"I'll go speak to her for a minute. I think she'll let you talk to her. I don't know whether she'll say anything in return."

She went down the hall to a closed door, knocked, and went in. It seemed to me she was gone a long time, but I was very sensitive about time and my judgments weren't too dependable. Eventually she came out, leaving the door open. She hesitated in passing, nodded her head once, then went on to her own room. I walked to the open door and looked in on Mary Carpenter.

The room was smaller than Miss Adams' room and there was a lot more furniture in it. There were a lot of things hanging on the walls, pennants, mottoes, and things like that. A disorderly wardrobe closet stood open. There was a three-quarter bed with the head against the middle of the far wall and on each side a high window with a window seat. Mary Carpenter was jackknifed on the one to the right of the bed. She had her back against one side, her knees up, and her bare feet braced against the other side. She was looking out the window into the big yard that surrounded the house.

What can I say, I was wondering, that will not cause her to stick her finger in her mouth?

"Miss Adams said you might talk with me a little," I said.

She started to put her finger in her mouth, changed her mind, and drummed with her fingers on her raised knees. They were round and fat-looking in the blue jeans.

"Okay," she said. "What do you want to talk about?"

Her voice had strength enough, but the way she threw the words together, swallowing about half of them, I had to strain to hear her.

What shall I say next? I thought.

On a dressing table, littered with feminine instruments, stood a framed, glass-covered photograph of a girl about seventeen or eighteen years old. She was pretty, with a thin, straight nose, a full, slightly twisted mouth, and large round eyes below a somewhat tousled head of blond hair. An inscription in a large round hand read: "To Mary with love, Esther."

"This is a picture of Esther Parrish?" I said.

She turned her head slowly and looked at me for the first time since I had entered. Then she looked at the picture for a while.

"Yes," she said. "Yeah. That's Esther."

"I'm sorry about her," I said.

She looked puzzled.

"Why?" she said.

"I'm sorry about what happened—that Peter killed her."

She looked away, out the window again.

"Oh," she said.

"I can't understand it. He must have been crazy."

She didn't say anything. After a minute she shrugged. "You must have known Peter pretty well," I said. "Did he do crazy things all the time?"

She moved her head, wrapped her arms around her knees, and finally decided to look at me again.

"He wasn't crazy," she said. "He was just like anybody else—except for his funny eyes."

"You mean his eyes were funny because they weren't straight? He was cross-eyed?"

"Yeah, that's what I mean," she said.

"Were they funny any other way?"

She shrugged fatly.

"I never looked at them that close," she said.

She giggled. I was developing an intense dislike for her and it was hard for me to hang on with the questions. I wished Miss Adams would come in and help.

But what could she do? I thought.

"I suppose you only saw him, Peter, that is, around school," I said.

"Sure, around school," she said.

"You and Esther."

"I wasn't always with Esther."

"Of course."

I wasn't getting anywhere. I had been through some frustrating inter-rogations in my time, but I couldn't remember any to equal this one.

"Well, thanks a lot," I said, turning away. "I won't take up any more of your time."

I headed for the door. I had meant it for a trick and it worked. It doesn't always work.

"Is that all you want to know?" she said.

She sounded in panic. I looked around and she had turned on the win-dow seat, put her feet on the floor, and was staring at me across the room. Her fingers dug at her knees.

I leaned in the doorway, looking at her.

"Well, I'd like to know more," I said, "but I don't want to upset you."

"It's all right," she said.

"Would you tell me a few things about that day you were riding with Esther and had the flat tire and Peter came along and took you into town to get it fixed?"

Her eyes moved this way and that.

"What kind of things?" she said.

"Anything you remember. Especially about Peter. How he behaved. Was he acting funny, crazy?"

"I told you he wasn't crazy," she said.

There is some goddam conspiracy in this town to keep saying Peter Davidian was not crazy, I thought. I heard it too much. He had to be crazy.

"All right. I forgot you said that," I said. "Let's see if I've got the facts straight. You and Esther had the flat tire out on the county road in the after-noon. It was a cold day. Peter came along in a pickup and started to change the tire, but the spare was flat and he put it in the truck and drove you and Esther into town to get it fixed. Right so far?"

"That's right," she said.

"The three of you hung around the service station while the tire was being fixed. What did you do to pass the time?"

That puzzled look clouded her face.

"What do you mean, what did we do? We just hung around. Drank a Coke, I guess. It didn't take very long."

"Well, you drank a Coke—out of the machine?"

"There's a Coke machine, yeah."

"Who put the money in? Who bought the Cokes? Peter?"

"I don't know. Somebody handed me a Coke. That's all I know. Peter never had any money. Esther probably bought the Cokes."

"And you got along all right, the three of you? You didn't split up and you and Esther go off by yourselves and leave Peter alone?"

"There wasn't any place to go."

"All right. So the three of you hung around there—what did you talk about? Tell jokes? Tease each other?" She shrugged.

"I don't know—Esther was always teasing Peter."

"Especially Peter? Did she tease other people too?"

"Well—boys. She used to tease them. They were always hanging around, bugging her."

"Trying to date her, things like that?"

"Yeah, sort of. She could have had any boy she wanted."

"But she didn't want any of them?"

She looked away quickly, her mouth tight. She hadn't meant to get into it that deeply.

"Anyway," I said, shifting ground, "you got back in the truck and drove out to Esther's car. And while Peter was trying to make the tire change, something went wrong with the jack. And he and Esther went off in the truck to drive to the Sampson farm so Peter could get another jack. You stayed in the car, waiting."

"Uh-huh, yeah."

"Why?"

"What do you mean why?"

"Didn't Peter offer to take you along in the truck too?"

"I don't remember. Maybe he did. But I didn't want to ride in the truck any more. It was rough and there wasn't room for the three of us in the seat."

"Why didn't Esther wait with you? Instead of going with Peter?"

"I don't know. Peter said he'd drive to the farm and get a jack, and Esther said, 'I want to go with you.' So Peter said all right and they went."

"And you waited about forty-five minutes for them to come back."

"At least. It seemed like years."

"It was cold out there?"

"Cold, and it was getting dark."

"What did you think about? Did you wonder why they didn't come back right away?"

"Well—sure, I wondered. I thought maybe Peter had a flat tire or something and they couldn't come right back. I got tired of waiting."

"So you got out and somebody came along and gave you a ride home."

"Yeah."

"Who? Who picked you up on the road?"

"Tony Bledsoe. He works for Esther's father."

"Oh yes, I remember. So he took you home."

"He took me home."

"Did you tell him why you were—hitchhiking?"

"No."

"Didn't he ask you why?"

"Not that I remember. But I didn't want to tell him anything about Esther. He might tell her father."

"What would there be about Esther that you wouldn't want her father to know?"

"Oh—I didn't mean it that way. I mean, it was getting late. Like that."

"I see. That would be the reason you wouldn't call Esther's father until nine o'clock that night."

"I wouldn't—what? I didn't call Esther's father. I was calling Esther—"

"Okay. What I really meant to ask was—did you have any kind of arrangement by which you would just—let me put it this way—if Esther wanted to be out somewhere in the evening and didn't want her father to worry about it, would you just let people take it for granted that she was with you, at your house or something like that?"

Her mouth opened and closed. She came up off the window seat as if it had suddenly turned into a hot stove burner.

"That's a dirty, nasty lie," she said. "You—you're just like all the others, trying to make Esther look bad. I'm not going to talk to you anymore. You get out."

A brief study was enough to convince me that she meant what she said. I had hit the raw nerve.

You should have known better, I told myself.

On the other hand, I thought, you have to try.

"All right," I said. "I'm sorry. I'll get out."

I didn't waste any time over it. When I stepped into the hall, Miss Adams was standing in the doorway to her bedroom. We looked at each other and I shrugged. She shook her head slightly and turned back into her room. I went down the stairs and found my way out of the house by the side door. There was no sign of Mrs. Carpenter. I wondered whether she had overheard any of my conversation with her daughter.

What about it? I thought.

And what about Mary Carpenter saying, "You're just like all the others"?

CHAPTER 7

It was a brisk six-minute walk downtown, but it felt good after the closed-in session with the neurotic girl. By the time I got to the hotel I was breathing freely and not too fast and my muscular tone had an easy tension, whereas a few minutes before it had been tight, not to say rigid. It appeared that something big was happening. There were many more cars on the street than I had seen at one time before, and knots of people clustered here and there on the sidewalks. I finally remembered that it was Saturday and the Saturday-evening crowd was gathering. Everywhere I looked people were making use of the town—in and out of the stores, the Wesley Café, lined up at the service stations. In the hotel lobby were about twenty people, mostly male, and a message for me that read: "Please call Sam Birch in Chicago."

Half a dozen of the twenty in the hotel lobby were gathered around the desk, chewing the fat with old Jess White-face. I couldn't hear myself talking to Sam Birch with their ears all around me.

"Listen," I said to Jess, "haven't you got a phone in the office I could use? I'll pay the charges."

His old white eyebrows twitched upward, then down.

"We got a telephone in there," he said. "Ain't supposed to use it except on hotel business. But if you got to be private—"

"I got to be private," I said firmly. "I hear better that way."

"Yeah—'course you do," he said.

During this exchange one of the loungers continued a monologue to which Jess nodded periodic assent. He crooked a finger at me and turned away, still nodding, and I found a way to get behind the desk and follow him. There was an office containing a battered oak desk, badly littered, a steel filing cabinet, and a safe big enough to serve the Chase Manhattan Bank on Friday afternoon at five o'clock. I wondered what was in it.

On the desk was a telephone. It was ivory white, and this was a shock at first until it occurred to me that it went well with Jess and the hotel atmosphere. There was a chance it was the only white telephone available to the local company.

"There 'tis," Jess said. "Help yourself. You can tell the operator who to charge it to."

"I promise I will," I said. "Thanks."

He nodded and made his ponderous way back to the desk, pulling the door almost, not quite, to. I let it go, picked up the phone, and placed the call to Sam Birch.

"Do you wish to wait, sir?" the operator asked.

"Yes," I said, "I'll wait."

"Very good, sir," she said.

I waited quite awhile. I could hear the call going through the various steps, from Wesley to the bigger county exchange, to Chicago and so on. Then when it seemed that Sam was about to come on the line there was an interruption of about three minutes, during which I gazed at the ceiling of the office and drummed a tune on the desk top with my fingers.

A new tone hummed on the line; there were clicks and I could hear Sam's voice, but it sounded very remote, as if he were calling from Tahiti or Tibet.

"Hello, Sam?" I said. "Mac. Returning your call."

"Yeah, Mac. Listen—"

"I can't hear you."

After a moment his voice returned, more clearly. "Okay, I closed the door. I'm down at the Stateville housing project," he said. "I got away earlier than I expected. I'm going to see Peter in a few minutes and I wanted to check with you."

"Oh. Well, this is how it's been going," I said. "People around here have got something stuck in their minds. Not only was Peter not crazy or even temporarily insane, he was very uncrazy. The trouble with it is, it makes sense."

"How sense?"

"Everybody is willing to let me think almost anything I want to about Esther Parrish—that she was a cute kid with a wild urge, that she probably fooled around and teased and generally made herself an agent of provocation. So—what if she did? What if she did it to Peter? What if he did the perfectly normal thing—killed her? What I'm trying to say is, if it was anything like that at all, she asked for it, and even if she did ask for it, he shouldn't have done it and he did too much, like cutting her up and all that, so he's dead."

"Watch your language, Mac."

"Sorry. This is a hard thing to get across—"

"I dig what you're saying. The thing is, what do we do? If you're about to give up, please let me know now, because the time is running out like it was Niagara Falls."

"I'm not thinking of giving up—though if you can find any stronger thing than me, don't hesitate to can me. But when you talk to Peter, ask him this: Ask him about hanging around the gas station that afternoon, waiting for Esther Parrish's tire to get fixed. Ask him how he felt, what Esther Parrish was doing, what Mary Carpenter was doing. Ask him who else was there, or came in and left again, whoever it was. Ask him every goddam detail you can think of about hanging around that gas station."

"All right, I've got that."

"What I'm thinking about," I said, "is when he started into the flip. If I can spot it at the gas station, maybe we can trace it up to the late evening. I don't know. It's just a grab in the wasteland."

"Good going. Anything else?"

"Just the stuff we talked about before, about working for Sampson and so on."

"Sure."

"I'm going to get something to eat and then start out again. I'll keep checking in."

"All right, Mac. I'll keep in touch."

I hung up. The door opened and Chris Duval pushed into the room, a vacuum cleaner in one hand and a dust rag in the other. He put his shoulder against the door, pushed it all the way to, and started his busy cleaning work. I stayed where I was at the desk, looking at the ceiling.

It must have been about five minutes before he began to talk. Now and then I would catch him sneaking a look at me. He started by humming, out of tune, under his breath, and gradually the humming turned into words, and after a while I could begin to make some of them out.

"…two-hundred and eighty-six chickens at the hatchery, Tuesday mornin', seven-thirty…"

Goddam it! I thought.

"That's a lot of chickens," I said, "all at once."

Chris didn't comment.

If I ask him a question, I wondered, will it blow the whole thing? Scare him off?

"I was talking to Mary Carpenter," I said to the ceiling. "Talking about Esther Parrish…"

I let it go at that. For a couple of minutes I thought it had been a mistake. Chris worked away with a kind of frantic dedication, his mouth tight-shut.

All that stuff he remembers, I was thinking, he must give it some significance. Esther Parrish is a scary thing to think about. He doesn't want to talk about it.

"…pretty," he said suddenly. "Pretty and proud—Esther Parrish. Good friend of Mary's. Smart too—talked French. *Parley-voo.* Miss Adams and Esther always talking French…teasin' all the time—try to get me to talk French. Hard to talk French, got to learn."

He stopped. I was getting the message—all he cared about was chickens and learning how to speak French.

"Esther got killed," I said. "Peter Davidian killed her."

It scared him. It was as if I had drawn a gun on him. He went stiff and his fingers squeezed down hard on his dust rag. His lips moved, but I couldn't hear anything. I couldn't decide whether to push it a little and maybe get him to spill over—or clam up for all time—or to let it go for now and hope the planting of the idea would break him open.

While I had been fretting, Chris had gone on talking. I heard him say:

"Never forget—right in there they was gettin' up the posse to look for her—Mr. Parrish, gatherin' fellas—George Medford, Bud White was there—that's old Bud—and Frank Judson—Tony Bledsoe—no, he come too late to git in on it—Saul Wright and Harry Ridenour—all of 'em—and Roscoe Embers swearin' 'em all in…"

The office door opened and big white Jess came in. It was his office and I couldn't very well ask him to get out. Chris was back at work, flicking here and there with his dust rag, when I got up from the desk.

"Thanks for the use of the phone," I said to Jess. "I waited a couple of minutes, thinking I might get a return call, but I guess not yet."

"Okay," Jess said. "Any time."

* * * *

The congestion at the hotel desk had eased off to three men in work clothes talking among themselves. There were maybe a dozen men here and there in the lobby and two or three women. It was ten after five by the lobby clock, and outside the street was jammed with cars crawling at odds, like disorganized ants. I climbed the stairs to my room, took off my jacket and shirt and tie, and washed up. I was drying myself when Caroline Adams' businesslike tread sounded in the hall.

I put on a fresh shirt and tie and after a suitable interval walked down to her door and knocked. There was a considerable waiting period, and then she opened up. She was wearing a bathrobe and slippers and pushing at her hair with her fingers.

"Wanted to thank you for helping me with Mary Carpenter," I said.

"That's all right. How did it go? Did you learn anything?"

"I'm not sure. Maybe a little."

"Well…"

We stood there. I knew I ought not to keep her standing around in her bathrobe, trying to make conversation, but I had the almost desperate feeling that if I couldn't hang onto her, everything was hopeless. She was the only solid help I had found, and she was getting to be a symbol of it.

"How about having dinner with me?" I said.

"I can't," she said. "Thanks just the same."

"Another date?"

"If it matters—yes."

"Whether it matters or not," I said, "I can't help thinking about it. None of my business, of course, but if it's with Mr. Parrish—he may not be in a real good mood."

She looked down at the backs of her folded hands, then up again.

"I think I can manage to take care of myself," she said.

"I'm sure of it," I said. "I hope you have a nice evening."

"Thank you."

I started away and turned back before she could close the door.

"I understand," I said, "that Esther Parrish spoke pretty good French, used to converse with you in French."

Her eyes blinked once slowly.

"Why, yes, we used to speak French once in a while. She wasn't really expert, but she was pretty proficient."

"And liked to show off?"

"I guess so. Most youngsters like to wear their accomplishments."

"Uh-huh," I said, backing off, "and I suppose there aren't many people in town she could speak French to and be understood."

"I guess not very many."

"Well, once again, have a good evening."

She nodded, backed into the room, and closed the door. I went down to my own room, got out my file on the Davidian case, and began to study the maps and the spotted locations, such as the Sampson farm, the abandoned farm where Esther Parrish had been murdered, the layout of the roads, and the time schedule that had been worked up by Sam Birch and his committee of psychiatrists.

I wonder what all those guys are doing now? I thought.

I heard Caroline Adams go down the hall to the bathroom and, sometime later, return. I put the maps and time schedule in my pocket, returned the rest of the file to a bureau drawer, and was getting into my jacket when there was a light rapping on my door. Caroline Adams was in the hall, dressed to go out and wearing a delicate, violet-like fragrance.

"Listen," she said, "how did you know about my speaking French with Esther?"

"Oh, I just picked up the information…"

"Not that it's a big secret, but I'm wondering who would be interested enough to mention it. Was it Mary?"

"No, it was Chris Duval."

She started to laugh.

"Chris? But—why? Did you ask him?"

"I didn't ask him anything. I just listened."

She stopped laughing, looked both ways along the hall, and did something with her fingers in her hair.

"Will you come in?" I said. "No need standing in the hall."

"I—only have a few minutes."

I pushed the door all the way open and she came in. There was nothing for her to sit on except the straight chair by the window. I started to sit down on the bed, changed my mind, and stood up. I had left the room door open. I couldn't think of anything else to put her at ease. "About Peter Davidian…" she said.

After a moment I said, "Yes. What about him?"

"Do you honestly believe he was—out of his mind when he—uh, did it?"

"I don't mean to be evasive," I said, "but what I believe doesn't really have anything to do with the problem. I'm trying to find out whether he was legally insane at the time."

"Legally insane," she said. "What does that mean?"

I shrugged.

"Who knows? A bunch of lawyers and psychologists."

"Then how can you investigate—how would you ever know—I mean, if you don't know what you're looking for?"

I shrugged again. There wasn't any reasonable answer. It was maybe like writing a poem.

"I'll just have to keep digging around," I said, "and hope it will work out. Maybe I'll recognize it when I see it, maybe not."

She looked rather broodingly at the window. Down in the street there was a sound of talk and rumbling gasoline engines.

"How much time do you have?" she said.

I counted on my fingers.

"About thirty-eight hours," I said. "The execution is set for eight in the morning, Monday."

She frowned and turned her face in a jerky way.

"He's so—young," she said.

"Yeah."

"Have you ever seen him? Peter?"

"No, I never have seen him."

"He had these odd eyes—crossed eyes. He was so quiet. He would sneak up on you."

"Literally sneak up—why?"

"No, I mean, you wouldn't realize he was around and suddenly he was there. He was like a—cat."

"How was he in school?"

She shook her head.

"Not very good. He never opened his mouth. His handwriting was almost impossible. He needed special help, but out here—"

Footsteps sounded on the stairs. Miss Adams appeared not to hear them. They reached the second floor, paused, then came on, and she got up suddenly.

"I'm afraid I'd better—" she said.

Then Jack Parrish was looking in at us.

"Hello, Jack," she said, moving toward the door.

"Ready?" he said.

"Yes, I'm ready."

"Good night," I said. "Have a good time."

She joined Parrish, who took her arm and walked her off down the hall. To judge by his manner, he hadn't considered me present. I hoped he wouldn't give her a rough time.

I checked one of my maps again, went down to the lobby, and checked in with Jess at the desk. There had been no return call from Sam Birch.

Outside I made my way among knots of pedestrians and parked cars across the street to the Wesley Café. A glance through the window was enough to discourage me. There were no vacant chairs, and people were standing around waiting. I estimated about an hour to get served. For the next thirty-eight hours I wouldn't have an hour to spare for eating.

I crossed back to the hotel side of the street and managed to ease my car into the stream of spasmodic traffic. It took me five full minutes to get from the hotel to the alley beside the town hall, a distance of one short block. The alley itself, happily, was unoccupied except for a couple of cars drawn up short of the beer joint where I had gone with Jack Parrish and Tony Bledsoe the night before. I pulled in behind the second car and walked to the tavern entrance.

CHAPTER 8

Like the café, the tavern was sold out but I remembered a large jar of pickled pigs' feet on the bar, and it is possible, in a pinch, to drink beer and eat pickles on your feet.

I pushed through a wiry mass of strong-smelling patrons at the bar and got some attention eventually. I ordered a glass and pointed to the jar, and the man delivered the beer and a pig's foot on a napkin. Then I had to push my way back through the press and find standing room on the dark side near the door. The good things about it were that the door was open, letting fresh air in, and that I could lean against the wall.

I was leaning there, gnawing at the pig's foot and sipping the beer, when Tony Bledsoe came in with two other mechanics. The three of them wore coveralls with the name "Jack Parrish—Int'l. Harvester" in black letters across their backs. One of them was the little guy I had seen Bledsoe come near to crushing under the garage hoist. The other was a rangy, well-set-up fellow, about Bledsoe's size, but looser and younger.

Bledsoe went the route I had taken to reach the bar, said something in a loud voice, and waited till the crowd opened up for him. He didn't have to wait long. The other two mechanics stood on the edge, waiting. Bledsoe returned with three bottles of beer and handed them over. Because there was no other direction for them to take, they moved toward where I was standing. Bledsoe finally caught sight of me and his face twisted in mock surprise.

"You still in town?" he said.

"Still here," I said.

I finished the skimpy end of the pig's foot and looked for a place to put it. There was no place, so I held it in my hand, wadded in the napkin.

"How you coming?" Bledsoe asked.

I shrugged. The other two stood around, drinking their beer, taking no special notice of me. Bledsoe dug at the little one with a greasy elbow.

"Fella from Chicago," Bledsoe said, "looking into the Peter Davidian case."

The small guy blinked at me. He was a man of fifty-five maybe, with a lined face and a harassed expression. I could understand the expression, if he spent much of his time under those grease racks.

"Yeah?" he said. "I thought Davidian was dead."

"Not yet," Bledsoe said. "Eight o'clock Monday morning."

I found some mild interest in the fact that he could rattle off the moment of execution that way. Then I decided there would be quite a few people around town who would have that moment in mind.

The second mechanic, whose name, according to the embroidery over his left pocket, was "Bud," swallowed a long pull of beer and said, "That guy was crazy."

I looked at him.

"Davidian?" I said.

He nodded.

"Nutty as a hot ox in fly time," he said.

Bledsoe was staring at him, holding his bottle between his belt and his chin.

"What the hell you talking about?" he said.

"I said he was crazy, nutty. Davidian, I'm talking about."

"The hell with him," the little mechanic said. "I got to get back. I don't finish that pickup tonight, Jack Parrish will take skin off me."

He tipped up his bottle and walked away, drinking from it as he went.

"Just when in Christ's name," Bledsoe said to Bud, "did you decide Davidian was crazy?"

"Had to be crazy," Bud said. "I always thought he was crazy."

The little mechanic came back from delivering his empty bottle and headed out of the tavern. He didn't look back at anyone on the way. Bledsoe turned away suddenly, banged his bottle down on a nearby table, and followed the little one. At the door he looked back to say:

"Come on. We got to finish that big one tonight. Jack promised it."

"Okay," Bud said and walked away.

I stayed where I was against the wall and drank the rest of my beer.

It could be a break, I thought. On the other hand, it could be that Bud was talking out of thin air.

However, I thought, if he has any evidence...

On the way to the car discouragement overwhelmed me.

He won't have any evidence, I thought. Nobody has any evidence. Peter Davidian is a dead man.

I got the car started, drove carefully to the end of the alley, turned and straightened, and headed for the county road.

* * * *

The spot where Esther Parrish had the flat tire was two and six-tenths miles from town, on the southwest corner of an intersection where a local road crossed the county highway. It took me just under five minutes to reach it, driving at a legal rate of speed.

I made a U-turn and pulled off on the shoulder, facing town, approximately in the position Esther's car would have been in while disabled. I sat there and tried to do some thinking. It was about an hour later than it would have been when Esther and the others had returned to put the good the on. It wasn't dark yet, but the sun had set. On the evening of the murder it would have been dark and it was cold. I couldn't imagine there had been much fooling around. The idea would have been to get that tire on so the girls could get home. It must have been quite a frustration when the jack went out.

All right, I thought, when the jack went out, Peter said he would drive to the Sampson farm and get another. I checked my map again and saw that the Sampson farm was about a mile and three-quarters from the scene of the flat tire.

It was nearly dark when I made another U-turn and drove north away from town to the next crossroad, a mile beyond the spot where the girls had had the flat tire.

I turned left, heading toward the Sampson farm, and within one minute passed the low-lying, shadowed rubble of the abandoned farm where Esther Parrish had been abused and murdered. In the momentary brilliance of early dusk I had a full view of the layout of the buildings, the fields around them, and the approach by the long, rutted lane. There was no cover. Even in full dark, I decided, anything as bulky as an automobile would have been in plain sight from the road, unless it had been hidden behind the crumbling chimney of the burned-out house, as mine had been on my first visit to the scene. According to Peter's story, he had looked into the barn that night because he had caught sight of Esther's car parked near it. This, I saw now, was perfectly believable.

It was not especially believable that Esther Parrish would have driven to the old barn voluntarily. The question of how she had got there, then, was as important as any. Unhappily, the simplest and therefore the most believable answer was that Peter had taken her there from the Sampson place and later had put the tire on her car and driven it to the barn and had been discovered before he had a chance to get away.

The thought about Peter Davidian made me look at my watch. I had that faintly stabbing sensation of fear, which was a recent habit with me, and had to force my mind to take note of the real time as I slowed and pulled up in front of the Sampson house. It had taken me about three minutes to make the trip from the spot on the county road where Mary Carpenter had sat waiting for Peter and Esther to return.

Mary had waited, she said, forty-five minutes. If I allowed five minutes for Peter to make the trip, another five to get the jack and put it in the truck, and another five to drive back, it still left half an hour unaccounted for. A good long time. Long enough.

It was dark now. I gazed at the high black windows in the porchless wall of the old house, trying to imagine what could have happened in that bad, long enough time. According to Peter, he had let Esther into the house so she could make some coffee and keep warm while he drove back to fix the wheel. But that didn't take care of half an hour.

Maybe Mary Carpenter didn't wait forty-five minutes, I thought. One minute can seem like ten when you're all alone and uncomfortable. Maybe she just picked forty-five out of the air. Because it was a number. Maybe it had only been fifteen minutes, or ten.

I wasn't getting anywhere. Even if I could dispose of the half-hour problem, there were too many other questions left. I started the car, backed into the Sampson lane to turn around, hesitated. I looked at the house for a minute, wondering whether there might be some answers inside it. Then I decided against breaking in for a search. The likelihood of finding anything after all this time was so slim, it would hardly be worth the time it would take.

Driving back down the road, I thought about that strongbox of Fred Sampson's, hidden in the old barn, the pathetic hoard of cash, the picture of Esther Parrish.

Fred Sampson, I thought, and slowed as I passed the abandoned farm. But the picture by itself didn't mean anything. Older men get fantastic notions about younger women, girls. Sampson might be quirky enough to indulge a secret passion, but he wouldn't be anyone Esther Parrish would go for. Would he?

Fifty yards beyond the old farm I pulled up and turned off my lights.

Who this time? I thought.

I counted to three, got out of the car, and walked back along the road to the lane that led to the murder barn. A big late-model car was drawn up facing the sagging door. I couldn't tell from the road whether anyone was inside it.

I walked down the lane, and the only sound was the crunching of my own footsteps in the dried grass between the ruts. I didn't hurry but kept going, reluctantly. The place might be a smoochers' haven and I didn't want to interrupt some random intimacy. It seemed an unlikely spot, though. You'd have to have a ghoulish kind of taste…

There was sudden, shadowy movement near the barn, then a man's shout.

"All right, by God, but now you know…!"

A slight figure ran to the car and reached for the door handle. I hesitated in the lane, fifty feet short of the car.

None of my business, I was thinking.

A larger figure appeared suddenly behind the smaller, reached, and jerked. The slight one fell away from the car, stumbling.

"Caroline, you listen to me…" the man's voice said.

I moved fast then down the lane. I could see clearly enough now. Caroline had recovered from the stumble and was standing some distance from the car, staring at big Jack Parrish who was beating with a loud fist at the car top. I stopped a few feet from him. He had to peer at me for a few seconds before he knew me. Then his fist stopped pounding.

"What the hell do you want?" he said.

I shrugged. "I heard a disturbance," I said.

"You heard a disturb—" he mumbled.

I didn't know what to do about him. For a couple of days to come I would have to be around town, investigating things he didn't want investigated. I had alienated him plenty already, and maybe a little more wouldn't matter. But maybe it would. Also, there was Caroline Adams to think about. If he didn't mean her any real harm, I couldn't help anybody by sticking my nose in. Still, he was upset and unpredictable.

"Would you like any assistance?" I asked Caroline, as neutrally as I could manage.

Parrish started toward me, moving stiffly as if his legs were in splints.

"You get around a lot, don't you?" he said.

I was looking most of the time at Miss Adams.

"No, I'm all right," she said after a minute.

"Okay," I said.

To take the pressure off the situation, I turned, ready to leave. Turning, I missed the warning of Parrish's lunge, and when one of his hard hands came down on my shoulder, I stumbled and turned only in time to see him coming for sure with a big fist cocked.

"Wait a minute!" he yelled.

I ducked when he threw the punch and stumbled again. There wasn't room enough to duck really, but he was muscle-bound and his reach was short. He went off balance, and I backed off some and waited till he got straightened out. I didn't want to fight him and I couldn't think of any words that might work on him.

"Hold it," I said.

"Jack, listen—" Caroline Adams said.

She shouldn't have said it. She was a woman and Jack Parrish was the wrong type for the application of feminine persuasion. He made a sound in his throat like the high-pitched growl of a nervous hound and came on again. Muscle-bound he was, but he had a lot of size on me and I knew I couldn't take the full impact of him. He had his right fist a little too high and I ducked under it and hit him under the ribs, twisting him a little. But the blow didn't faze him; he swung with the other hand and banged my right ear. My head buzzed and I stepped into a rut and fell on my back. Happily there was only grass where my head hit.

He was standing over me, waiting for me to get up. Once more I tried talking.

"I got no beef here," I said, looking up from my elbows.

"I got a beef," he said. "Get up."

Vaguely behind him I saw Caroline Adams in motion.

Stay all the way out of it, lady, I prayed.

I never did know whether she stayed out of it or not, but it didn't matter any more. Parrish stooped and reached for my jacket, and I didn't have any more time to think about things. I managed to get my feet up and kick at his knees. He sprawled down over me, and I kicked my way free of him and got on my feet running. When I turned back, he was charging again. I could hear the breath racking in his throat. My head hurt but had stopped buzzing. I let him get in close, side-stepped, and hit him hard in the stomach, high under his diaphragm. His weight pushed me back fast and I kept my feet under me by sheer luck. He swung wild and caught my shoulder, throwing me to one side. He was big as a house and I couldn't cut him down with my hands.

He was wheezing, gasping for air, and I got my head down, pushed hard with my right foot, and slammed my shoulder into his midriff, where I had hit him before. He sagged and backed off and I followed through. One open hand landed on my ear as I went in, but I got my shoulder into him all right. He couldn't breathe any more then. He turned on his feet slowly, his face lifted, looking for air. I aimed the heel of my hand at his head behind his left ear, then held back as he toppled onto his face in the lane. I had a fuzzy awareness that Miss Adams was hovering near us, but I didn't try to find her.

Parrish was in a bad way, face down, but with his neck stretched, as if he had to find the moon and didn't know where to look. I straddled him, got hold of his belt and pulled up, let down, pulled up again, giving him some rough-and-ready artificial respiration. I was scared. I didn't know what I'd do if I'd hurt him too much to bring him around.

After about three hard pumpings up and down he squirmed and kicked at me, trying to get away. I knew he'd be all right then. I walked away, gulping to catch some breath of my own. Miss Adams was standing near the back end of the car, bracing herself against it with one hand. I noticed it was a Cadillac.

"Can you drive it?" I asked her.

"What?"

"The car—do you know how to drive it?"

"Oh—I guess so. It's all automatic."

"Take mine if you'd rather. Somebody will have to drive him to town. He won't be in shape for a few minutes."

"All right."

"I'll load him in the back seat. You drive to town, to his house. I'll follow you. If he gives you any trouble, blink the lights and stop the car."

"No—he won't. Are you all right?"

"Sure, I'm fine. Sorry about the mess."

"It wasn't your fault. How did you know we were here?"

"Saw you from the road—the car, I mean."

I went to Parrish. He was still on the ground, but he had turned over, drawn his knees up, and was concentrating on breathing. It was smart of him.

"Will you open the left rear door?" I said to Caroline Adams.

She moved quickly around the end of the car. It took her a while to get the door open, but she made it.

"Maybe you could back it along here closer," I said. "He's a big one."

That took some more time. The car lights went on, the motor rumbled, and she backed slowly, leaning out of the seat to see where she was going. The car lurched over the ruts and came to a stop. I got hold of Parrish's hand and arm, pulled him up some, and worked his head and shoulders inside the open car door. By then he could help a little, not much. He turned over, pushed with his feet, and I boosted him from behind. He sprawled on the back seat. I jackknifed his legs to get them into the car and slammed the door shut.

The exertion had winded me, and I leaned against the door by the wheel, catching my breath.

"Where's your car?" Miss Adams asked me.

"Just up the road. Give me a couple of minutes, then back out, or turn around, and drive to town. He'll be all right by the time he gets home. I'll follow you. I'll pick you up at his place and drive you downtown."

"You don't have to—"

"I have to insist. Drive carefully."

I pushed away from the car and started up the lane to the road. It was hard going at first, but I was all right by the time I hit the pavement.

CHAPTER 9

Parrish lived on a miniature estate at the north end of town. There was a whitewashed stake-and-rider fence around maybe a full acre of tree-covered grounds, and a long winding drive led to a garage beside a low, rambling wood-and-stone ranch house. There was a dim light inside the house. Miss Adams had stopped the Cadillac on the drive at a side door. I pulled up behind. When I walked to Parrish's car, he was sitting up on the back seat, staring straight ahead. I opened the front door and helped Miss Adams out.

"Just stand right here for a minute," I said.

I went around the car, opened the rear door, and looked in.

"You want any help into the house?" I asked.

He turned his face very slowly, his neck swelling with the effort, and looked at me.

"Just get out," he said hoarsely. "Get away from me."

"All right," I said. "Good night."

I walked back to where Miss Adams was waiting. "Come on," I said. "Let's go."

She hesitated, peering into the car.

"Is he all right?" she asked.

"Yeah, he's all right."

"Should I call a doctor or something?"

"You can call from the hotel if you want to. He can call. He can talk all right. I just tested him."

Finally she decided to come along. I opened the door for her and she got in, and I went around and got under the wheel, backed down Parrish's drive to where I could turn, and got headed for the hotel. Miss Adams sat in silence until I asked:

"What happened out there at the barn?"

"I don't—it was so strange. We were going to drive over to the county seat for dinner, and all of a sudden he turned off the road and went to that—place."

"No warning at all?"

"No warning. He just drove to the old farm, stopped, and made me get out. Then he took me in the barn and started talking about Esther and Peter—he was wild. There was nothing I could do or say. He just raved."

"What did he rave about mostly?"

"About the—tragedy. Mostly about Peter. He said he wasn't going to get cheated. He missed one chance, he said, to pay Peter for Esther's murder, and he wouldn't miss it again—that was what he raved about."

"Anything else? Anything about me?"

"Well, he mentioned you."

"What did he call me?"

"I'd rather not say."

I had to slow down on the edge of the business street for the Saturday-night traffic, which was heavier than it had been earlier, and slower. There were pedestrians all over the street, and it took concentration to make my way through them in the car.

"I feel it was really my fault," Miss Adams said, "what happened between you and Jack, I mean. I shouldn't have been in your room when he came for me."

"Wasn't your fault," I said.

There wasn't any place to park near the hotel. I drove to the town hall, turned up the alley and went to the back street, around the corner, and pulled into a slot about a block from the hotel on the side street.

"We both need to do a little brushing up," I said. "If you'll give me a few minutes to change, I'll buy you some dinner and we can have a talk."

"I really don't feel hungry…"

"You have to eat whether you're hungry or not. And it's time to do some talking."

She didn't say anything but walked along all right to the hotel and into the lobby. The earlier crowd had dwindled. There were a couple of farmers chewing the fat off in one corner, and in the middle of the lobby on one of the sofas a man in a business suit was sitting straight upright, his knees together, supporting a black brief case. He didn't belong. He was from far off somewhere.

Miss Adams and I paused at the desk to pick up keys, and the man on the sofa got up and walked over.

"You're Mac?" he said.

I nodded.

"Yeah," I said. "I'm Mac."

"I'm Doctor Prentiss," he said. "I have some material from Sam Birch to go over with you."

"You're one of the group?" I asked.

"Yes."

"Miss Adams," I said, "this is Doctor Prentiss."

He nodded.

"Miss Caroline Adams?" he said.

She blinked a couple of times and nodded.

"Yes, how do you do?" she said.

Prentiss was looking me over furtively. I brushed at my stained, wrinkled jacket, made an effort to straighten my tie.

"We had a little fuss with another fellow," I said. "We haven't had any dinner. Have you?"

"I had a snack. I flew into the county seat and rented a car to get here."

"Well, come on up. We'll change and then we can all go somewhere and see to things."

He didn't seem to object to my pushing. I could have been more polite, but I was damned if I'd let Caroline Adams get away again. This might be the time she could be really useful.

The three of us went to the stairs and up to our floor. I nodded to Miss Adams, who went on ahead to her own room. I unlocked my room, showed Dr. Prentiss in, gave him a chair, and started to change my clothes.

"What was the nature of the fuss?" he asked.

I told him about it hurriedly.

"That's too bad," he said.

"I know it," I said. "I'm sorry, but it just happened to work out that way and I did the best I could with it."

"I'm sure you did."

"What have you got from Sam?"

"A transcript of his talk with Peter Davidian this afternoon."

"Good," I said.

There was a mirror over the chest of drawers, and I saw that I was more of a mess than I had realized.

"Be right back," I said. "I'll go down the hall and wash up some."

I was in the bathroom for about five minutes. It wasn't too bad, once I scraped the dirt off. There were a couple of lumps on my head, a bruise on my right cheekbone, and at least three very sensitive bruises on my chest. My ear was still more or less numb, but I could hear all right.

When I got back to the room, Dr. Prentiss had opened his brief case and taken out some papers. I was opening a fresh shirt when he said:

"Has Miss Adams been any help?"

"Not much yet—well, some. I think she can be more help and I hope within the next couple of hours."

"Do you want to run through this transcript now?" he said.

I thought about it.

"Anything sensational in it?"

"I don't know for sure. Maybe, maybe not. It's hard to evaluate."

"Let's save it for dinner. I'd like Miss Adams to be in on it."

"All right. Have you talked with Mary Carpenter?"

"Yeah, finally. Not much came of it."

"You've run into hostility, obstruction?"

"Uh-huh. Jack Parrish is the town boss, as far as I can see, and he calls most of the shots."

He made an overprecise gesture with thin, straight lips.

"This little altercation with him tonight may make it even rougher," he said.

"Yeah. Listen, will you level with me?"

"Certainly."

"You really, honestly believe that Peter Davidian was legally insane when he killed Esther Parrish?"

The gesture again. He was one of those guys who is all brain and it was hard for him to relax with me, especially in my beat-up condition.

"We don't acknowledge the legal definition," he said. "We think that Peter Davidian was so emotionally disturbed that he was not responsible for his actions to the extent that he ought to be executed."

"What's emotionally disturbed?"

He didn't have to feel around for the answers.

"In his case," he said, "it's a condition in which he couldn't control an impulse because an accumulation of rage and frustration had caused him to lose touch with his own check points, as I call them."

I thought about that while I got my tie on.

"How come that didn't come out at the trial?" I asked.

"Partly because the witness wasn't very strong, partly because of the nature of the act—the jury was too horrified to listen to any reason. Usually when it's so obvious, as in Peter's case, it comes out all right. This time it didn't."

"You say it's obvious," I said, reaching for my coat, "but around town here nobody seems to feel that way. The thing I hear most of all is 'he wasn't crazy.'"

"Well," he said, stuffing the papers back into his bag, "around town feeling still runs high and the local experts aren't awfully qualified."

"Hmn," I said.

I opened the door and went down to Miss Adams' room.

"Just a minute," she said when I knocked.

I went back to my room and stood in the open doorway while Dr. Prentiss checked his appearance in the mirror.

"How's Peter's morale?" I asked.

He shrugged lightly.

"I suppose it's about what you'd expect," he said.

I had the uneasy feeling he didn't really care very much. It seemed to me to be a thing worth caring about.

As he joined me at the door, he asked, "Where will we be going for dinner? I chartered a flight to the county seat. I told the pilot I'd be ready for the return trip at about eleven. Heavy schedule tomorrow."

"There's a place outside of town, not far," I said.

"Good."

Miss Adams came out of her room, gazed at us for a moment, then locked her door and came along. We descended to the lobby in a slightly ridiculous silence.

* * * *

For the short ride to the Glade Dr. Prentiss rode in back, by his own choice. There wasn't any conversation until I had got through the traffic and out on the road, heading west. Miss Adams was twisting her hands in her lap in a kind of rhythmic, compulsive way, and I felt obligated to ease the tension.

"There's a fellow works for Mr. Parrish," I said, "by the name of 'Bud.' Do you know him?"

"I guess not. I think I've heard the name," she said, "but I wouldn't know what he looks like."

"Tall, well-built fellow, young, younger than Tony Bledsoe, I think."

She shook her head.

"Reason I ask," I said, "earlier this evening I happened to get into a conversation with Bledsoe and this Bud and another mechanic from Mr. Parrish's place, and along the line Bud said Peter Davidian was crazy."

She sat still, looking straight ahead. After a while Dr. Prentiss cleared his throat in the back seat.

"Did you talk to him about it?" he asked.

"Not yet. No chance. Bledsoe didn't like it that he made the remark. They all cut out and that was that."

"Might be worth following up," Prentiss said.

I was getting unfond of him.

"Yes, sir," I said.

He didn't say any more.

"When I came down the lane tonight," I said, "you ran to the car and Jack Parrish followed you, and I heard him say, 'All right, but now you know.' What did he mean by that?"

She twisted her hands in her lap.

"He had been talking—" she said, and stopped.

"Raving?"

"Well—half raving, not entirely. He had been saying that people—that is, you—were trying to make out that Peter Davidian was crazy, trying to get him off from the—uh—execution."

"I see," I said. "What then?"

"Well, he kept saying over and over to me that Peter wasn't crazy at all, and finally I kind of broke down and said, 'Please stop—I just don't know whether he was crazy or not. I don't know!' And then—he told me that the day before the murder, Peter had driven into the garage—Jack's garage—and he wasn't upset or acting funny or anything, and he said to Tony—Tony Bledsoe—that Jack better do something about Esther or she would be killed."

"That was when you ran out of the barn?"

"Yes."

"And that's why he came out, yelling that 'now you know.'"

"That's the way it happened."

"He didn't have any interpretation of what Peter told Tony Bledsoe?"

"No—that is—maybe I didn't give him time."

I glanced into the back seat momentarily.

"I don't remember that threat being mentioned in the trial," I said, "if it was a threat."

"No," Dr. Prentiss said. "It would be questionable evidence. Hearsay. It could be admissible, but there would be a lot of hesitation about it, and maybe the prosecutor thought he had enough without it."

"Hearsay?"

"Yes," he said. "It seems that Bledsoe was the only person who heard the remark and he didn't testify at the trial."

"Why not?" I said.

I hadn't noticed that in the trial transcript. I had just been taking it for granted that everybody in town who knew anything at all had testified—except Chris Duval, who probably didn't really know anything, except how many chickens were hatched out from time to time and when it was somebody's birthday.

"Disqualified," Dr. Prentiss said. "He was a convicted felon."

"For what?" I said.

"Forgery—several years ago."

I pulled into the parking area at the Glade and Caroline Adams said quietly:

"That's true. Jack Parrish gave him a break after Tony had served six months in prison, gave him a job. Tony's very devoted to Jack, naturally."

I turned off the switch, helped Miss Adams out of the car, and the three of us went into the restaurant. Since we wanted to look at the transcript of Sam's talk with Peter Davidian, we went into the dining room, where there was light enough to read by.

When we were seated, Dr. Prentiss excused himself and Caroline Adams leaned far across the table, looking unhappy.

"Listen," she said, "I don't know what I'm doing here. I'm very uncomfortable and I'm not hungry, and after all that's happened—"

"I know," I said. "I appreciate it that you came at all. I need your help. And so does Dr. Prentiss."

"Who is he?"

"One of my bosses. I never met him before. Probably a psychiatrist or psychologist. He has some stuff for me to look over. If you can stick it out, I'll be indebted to you."

"Well—I—just feel so strange and confused."

"So do I. Have a drink."

"That might help."

We decided what we would have to drink, and Dr. Prentiss got back in time to say he wouldn't care for one. I got a little more unfond of him.

"How long a talk did Sam have with Peter?" I asked. Dr. Prentiss opened his brief case.

"Not very long. That is, the time was adequate, but Peter didn't have much to say."

"We might as well get started on it," I said.

Dr. Prentiss pulled out a slim sheaf of typescript and laid it on the table. Our drinks came and he asked the waitress for a glass of tomato juice. Caroline Adams and I were sitting next to each other, so we could read the pages at the same time. The transcriber had done a good job. The conversation had been recorded on tape and the typist had filled in pauses, so we had a fairly accurate picture of how it had gone.

There wasn't much on the first two or three pages:

> Q. (MR. BIRCH): Hello, Peter, how are you feeling?
> A. (DAVIDIAN): *(No answer)*
> Q. Is there anything you need that you want me to ask for?
> A. *(Pause)* No—thanks—guess not.
> Q. I brought you a message from Mrs. Sampson. She says she misses you and to keep your spirits up and to pray every night.

A. *(Pause)* Yeah—well—thanks.

It went on like that for a couple of pages more, as if Sam had kept trying to get Peter interested in something and Peter kept evading him. Even in the hard black lines of the type you could see that the morale was very low.

On page 3, near the bottom, Sam began trying to cheer him up by telling him how hard we were working on the case and talking to all the people who had known Peter, giving me an exaggerated build-up and so on. But there was no solid material on page 4. Peter was non-committal. Once he said, "Not much chance, I guess."

Sam had said: "There's always a chance. Don't give up."

"It's all right," Peter said. "I don't care."

Caroline Adams read with concentration. I noticed her left hand gripping the edge of the table, the knuckles of her slim fingers whitened, the joints concave with tension.

Along about the middle of page 5 Sam had begun to bear down.

Q. Peter, you could help us. This detective, Mac, has some things he wants to know about and he thought you could tell him. One of the things was about what happened at the gas station that afternoon when you went in to get Esther's tire fixed.

A. *(Pause)* What happened? What do you mean? Nothing happened special. Just hung around waiting.

Q. Well, did you—I mean you, Peter—just sit there in the truck and not say anything or see anybody—just sat there and waited?

A. Oh, folks would come in and go away—like in a gas station. I don't remember too good—didn't do anything.

Q. How were you feeling while you waited? What were the girls doing?

A. Well, I don't know—just fooling around, had a Coke or something...

Q. Did they get you a Coke too?

A. Yeah, I think so—I guess they did.

Q. Were you bored, or worried about anything? Because you were spending all that time?

A. *(Pause)* No—you know—uh-uh. I didn't have anything else...

Q. Did the girls tease you or anything?

A. *(Pause)* What...? *(Pause)* No—I don't remember—I didn't pay much attention—

Q. They didn't get you upset or sore at them for any reason?

A. I don't know—what you would call they didn't bother me none.

And so it went. I was beginning to understand what Sam meant when he said Peter wasn't talkative. When I flipped the page over, Caroline Adams turned her face and looked at me with an odd expression. It was a mixture of anguish and curiosity, almost a tortured look. I tried to smile, but it didn't feel right.

About three seconds later the hand that had been gripping the table lifted, her fist clenched, then opened, and she put her index finger on the page about a third of the way down from the top.

> Q. Peter, will you tell me something about Mary Carpenter?
>
> A. No. Leave me alone. I don't want to talk about her.
>
> Q. Why not, Peter?
>
> A. Because—naturally—I don't. She was her—Esther was her best friend, see—
>
> Q. That's why I'm asking. How did you feel about Mary Carpenter?
>
> A. I—look, do I have to talk about—
>
> Q. No, you don't have to talk about anything. But you can help us, and maybe yourself, too, if you will.
>
> A. *(Long pause)* Mary liked me, you know—Esther didn't treat her right...
>
> Q. And you liked Mary?
>
> A. Nah—always giggling—she made me nervous.

Miss Adams had put her finger on the answer that read: "Mary liked me..." She hadn't moved it. I looked at her and she was nodding.

"True," she said. "Mary told me."

I glanced at Dr. Prentiss.

"Mary told you that she liked Peter?" I said.

"Yes," Miss Adams said. "But of course that was—before—"

Prentiss made his way into the conversation.

"Did she like him in a way that caused her disturbance?"

"I don't know about that," Caroline Adams said. "Sometimes she seemed to be disturbed about—well—I don't know."

"About what?" I said.

"I—just don't know for sure."

"Was Mary disturbed about the way Esther treated Peter?" I asked.

"I—I don't know how Esther treated Peter."

"Do you know any hearsay about it?"

"Only from Mary—"

"What I'm trying to get at," I said, "is what Mary thought about Esther and Peter—if there was anything to think about."

"I don't know that there was."

She was firm-lipped. But studying her face, I didn't think she was being evasive.

I went back to the transcript:

> Q. Did Esther Parrish make you nervous?

A. (Pause) Well— (Pause—no answer)

Q. Did Esther tease you—call you names?

A. We talked about all this before.

Q. All right, Peter, take it easy. I won't push you. I just want you to tell us anything you can remember about that day—around the gas station, anything Mary did or Esther—or anybody who came into the station while you were waiting...

A. I don't know—I just can't remember—

Q. Anybody come in and talk to the girls, to Esther?

A. Everybody was always talking to Esther.

Q. And that day too, while you were waiting around the gas station?

I looked up and met Prentiss' eye. "Good old Sam," I said. "He never quits."

Prentiss nodded.

A. Well, different people would come in, to get gas, stuff like that—like people do—and Esther—she was telling everybody about me—because I was helping her get the tire fixed. She would—ahh—it's crazy.

Q. Why don't you just tell me and let me decide whether it's crazy?

A. She would tell people, "I'm in love with him"—meaning me—"because he's so nice to me. As soon as he gets a place of his own"—meaning a farm like—"I'm going to marry him."

Q. She said—she told everybody who came in that she was going to marry you.

A. Not everybody—different ones.

Q. Can you think of any of them—any at all?

A. Well—no—maybe one or two—see, I don't know many people in town, only to look at. I don't know their names. There was a guy from Jack Parrish's garage—a mechanic—little scrawny guy named Amos. I knew him because he did some work for Mr. Sampson, on his tractor.

Q. Amos. Anybody else you remember?

A. Not by name. There was a girl worked for the telephone company, then there was—different ones, I don't know their names.

Q. All right, you take it easy there a minute, Peter. I'm going to get us a couple of Cokes or something. You like Coke all right?

A. I guess so, fine—thanks...

It was the bottom of the page. I looked up and wondered suddenly why we weren't getting any service. Caroline Adams was sipping at her drink. She seemed to have some trouble swallowing. When I looked at her eyes, they glistened faintly.

"What time is it?" I asked.

Caroline Adams set her drink down a little too hard, spilling some of it. Dr. Prentiss' eyes flicked from her to me and went away. I lifted my hand and signaled a waitress, who nodded impatiently.

"One of the things to remember," Dr. Prentiss said, "is that some people can take more teasing than others. A boy like Peter, with the handicap of the internal strabismus—crossed eyes—is likely more sensitive than many others. The fact is Peter is extremely sensitive, to the point of being continually anxious."

The waitress came and I asked Miss Adams what she would have.

"Nothing, thanks," she said. "I would like another drink."

"All right, but eat something too. What kind of soup do you have?"

"Chicken gumbo," the waitress said.

"Two big bowls, and I'll have a ham sandwich."

Dr. Prentiss ordered a vegetable plate and a glass of non-fat milk.

I turned the page of the transcript and read some more. Miss Adams appeared to have lost interest.

> Q. You're helping a lot, Peter. Can you tell me how you felt about that—about what Esther was telling people, about you—
>
> A. Well, she was just teasing, you know. She didn't mean it.
>
> Q. All right, she was teasing. How did you feel about it? Did you get mad?
>
> A. No—she was always saying something like that—
>
> Q. About you personally, or just about everybody?
>
> A. About me.
>
> Q. Did she tease you in other ways? Fool around?
>
> A. I don't know what you mean.
>
> Q. Well, I mean, for instance, would she flaunt herself—make herself—oh, sexy—and lead you on?
>
> A. Nothing like that—no—
>
> Q. Did you ever think about her that way? Privately? In your own mind?
>
> A. *(Pause)* Did I…? *(Pause)* She was a real pretty girl, you know. She wouldn't care about somebody like me—
>
> Q. But in your own head, did you ever think about her in that way?
>
> A. Oh—maybe—once in a while—
>
> Q. And about other girls?
>
> A. I don't remember—
>
> Q. About Mary Carpenter?
>
> A. Mary…? Gosh, no! She was so funny—

I glanced at Miss Adams, who was concentrating on her drink exclusively. The waitress brought the soup and Dr. Prentiss' vegetable plate and went away for the rest of the order.

"Good soup," I said.

Dr. Prentiss nodded. Miss Adams didn't say anything. I returned to the transcript, which was running out of pages.

Q. There's one other thing I'd like to talk about, Peter. I know we've been over it before, but about the Sampsons, and you working and living there—what was it like?

A. *(Pause)* Oh—it was just—living and working. I had a roof over my head. They fed me good.

Q. You worked pretty hard, didn't you?

A. Well—farm work is rough.

Q. Did you ever get angry at Fred Sampson? Angry enough to fight him?

A. Fight...! What are you talking about? How could I fight him? He was taking care of me. After my father died—

Q. I know—the Sampsons took you in. But didn't you ever get real upset and mad, because you had to work so hard and you didn't have much of a life out there, all by yourself...?

A. Everybody gets mad sometimes. I would get mad about something, but not at the Sampsons. That would be wrong.

Q. When you did get mad at something, what would you do? Swear? Throw things?

A. Oh—different things, depending how mad I was—you know—

Q. But you never got mad at Fred Sampson.

A. No—not like—no I never did.

Q. Did Fred Sampson ever talk to you about the girls, Esther, Mary?

A. Talk to me...? About what?

Q. I remember you told me about the girls sometimes coming out and hanging around the farm while you were working. Did Esther tease you then?

A. *(Pause)* Oh—sometimes.

Q. Did Fred Sampson ever get angry because they were hanging around, keeping you from your work?

A. Well—he chased them off a couple times.

Q. Did you get angry about that?

A. No—not at him.

Q. I see. Well—one more thing. That afternoon, after you got back from having the tire fixed, and you found Esther's jack wouldn't work, you and Esther drove to the farm, to get another. And Esther decided she'd wait in the house while you went back—make some coffee.

A. Yeah, that's right.

Q. So you let her in the house. You showed her where the coffeepot was and cups and so on, and you went out and found the jack and put it in the truck.

A. Uh-huh.

Q. And then what did you do?

A. What...? I drove back to the car and put the tire on. Then I went back to get Esther.

Q. And when you got to Esther's car, you saw that Mary was gone.

A. Yeah.

Q. And after you got the tire changed, you drove back to the farm and Esther was gone.

A. Right—yeah.

Q. Where did you think she had gone?

A. I didn't know. She was—you never could tell about her.

Q. Did you try to figure it out? Did you think she'd gone off somewhere on foot, on a cold evening like that?

A. I don't know—she might have. I didn't think about it much.

Q. Was there any sign that anything had happened in the house while you were gone?

A. No. It was kind of messy, because she made the coffee and didn't clean up. I cleaned up after her, drove back and put the keys in her car, and drove to town to get something to eat.

Q. And none of this made you angry? That you had gone to all that trouble and Esther made coffee without cleaning up and then disappeared and you had that extra traveling and all that—you weren't upset with her?

A. I don't know—maybe a little. She was always like that—you couldn't depend...you never could tell. *(Pause)*

Q. Listen, Peter—when you told this in court, the jury didn't believe you.

A. I know.

Q. You know why?

A. No—I—look, I don't remember everything—

Q. The reason the jury didn't believe it was because you didn't believe it yourself.

A. I—told you—

Q. Listen, you don't have to be afraid to tell everything. If you tell us now, we can do something about it.

A. I don't—I can't talk about it any more.

Q. All right, that's enough for now, Peter. If you want anything, you know how to go about it. I'll be in close touch with you. And we'll keep working.

A. It's all right. It don't matter—

Q. Yes, it does. You keep your chin up now. Don't get discouraged.

A. Yeah—all right. Goodbye...

That was the end of the transcript. I flipped over the page, took a spoonful of lukewarm soup, and looked at the ham sandwich on the side plate.

"'Don't get discouraged,'" I said.

Caroline Adams looked at me, then looked away. Dr. Prentiss finished the last of his vegetables.

"You think Peter is holding something out?" I asked. He shrugged.

CHAPTER 10

"What did the jury believe?" I asked.

I had read it, but I wanted to hear it from Prentiss. I had a feeling I didn't know anything about him, and he was one of the experts and I owed it to him to find out how they were thinking. He owed it to me to let me in on it.

He pushed his plate aside, leaned on his elbows and said, with precision:

"The jury believed that Peter let Esther into the house to make coffee and that he made advances to her. This would account for the time Mary Carpenter waited in the car. Esther repulsed him and he lost his temper and killed her. So far—manslaughter, second-degree murder. But Peter wasn't finished. He had the dead girl on his hands and it was necessary to dispose of her. He put her in the truck and drove to the abandoned farm. He put her in the barn, went to her car, and changed the tire. Then he drove her car to the old barn and left it. He walked back across the fields to his truck, drove into town, and had dinner. And then, on his way home that night, he stopped at the barn and, once more consumed with rage, he performed the atrocities that turned the second-degree murder into an unpardonable outrage. This is what the jury believed, as well as every court of appeal."

"And what do you—what does the group believe?"

"As for the facts, we believe that is what happened. It is virtually inevitable. It makes perfect sense. But we also believe that Peter was in an emotional condition under which he should not have been held responsible to the point of execution."

"Is there an issue of capital punishment?"

He put his hands together, looked at them, put his face in them, then looked up over them.

"No issue of capital punishment," he said. "If we have views on capital punishment, they're not relevant to this case. We believe that execution in this particular case would be a miscarriage of—public responsibility. We believe Peter can be treated so as to become an emotionally balanced member of society."

"Well," I said, "what evidence do you have on his emotional condition at that time? I haven't been able to find any. What did you start with?"

He shifted in his chair and dropped the bookish tone.

"We ran a batch of tests on him. Some of the best men in the field. We worked him over from top to bottom. The tests show that his actions were predictable. Unfortunately a girl like Esther Parrish wouldn't be able to predict them.

"Besides the tests, there were some circumstances in Peter's early life and in his life with the Sampsons that made the affair of Esther Parrish perfectly logical as an outcome of his behavior patterns."

Caroline Adams was sitting back in her seat with her face down, her hands in her lap. I felt she was listening, but I wasn't sure.

"I know it must sound very dogmatic and remote to you," Dr. Prentiss said, "but it's solid stuff and it's what we've got. We need more, obviously. That's where you come in."

I looked at him for a while and thought wistfully of a couple of quiet, cool places in Chicago where it would be peaceful and comforting, if only I could get there before closing. Then I pushed back from the table, picked up the tab, and said:

"All right, let's get out of here and I'll get back to work."

Dr. Prentiss reached across the table and plucked the tab out of my hand.

"Please," he said.

"Okay," I said.

I helped Caroline Adams out of her chair and we left the place. During the drive back to town Dr. Prentiss sat in front with Miss Adams and me. It was more friendly, but it seemed to me that it made her uncomfortable. Once I almost stopped to ask him to get in back but decided against it. I was too tired for that kind of stuff.

We pulled up around the corner from the hotel and walked back. The crowd had thinned somewhat and there weren't any massed pedestrians. It was after ten o'clock and getting past bedtime.

A couple of tall, stooped guys in overalls were standing on the hotel steps as we climbed them and they broke off their conversation and watched as we passed. I couldn't see us with their eyes and it annoyed me. I yanked at the thin metal handle of the screen door and it came off in my hand. I tossed it away, got my fingernails in place, and got the thing open. The lobby appeared to be deserted, except for old Jess sitting white-faced at the desk. Caroline Adams started across the lobby, moving quickly toward the stairs. Halfway home she stopped, looked around, then drifted to one side and hovered like an addled bird. I took about six steps toward her and pulled up. Dr. Prentiss stood around uncertainly while I gazed at my luggage, neatly strapped and latched, in a neat assembly on the lobby floor.

I glanced at Caroline Adams, looked over my shoulder at Prentiss, and went to the desk. Jess's head was bent over a newspaper. He was shading his white brows with pale hands cupped.

"What?" I said.

It took him about fifteen seconds to look up.

"Eh—oh," he said, "it's you."

"What about my luggage?"

He shifted ponderously and peered around me into the lobby.

"Oh yeah," he said.

He reached under the desk and brought up a slip of paper with numbers on it. My bill.

"No rooms available," he said, as if he had learned it off a record. "Sorry."

I was badly bugged by now and my control was not all the way on. My voice rose.

"What do you mean no rooms? Besides me you got one other tenant in this fleabag."

His brows twitched.

"Got remodeling to do," he said. "Fellas starting right soon now."

"In the middle of the goddam night?" I shouted.

"Wouldn't be surprised," he said.

I had my mouth open to mouth a few strong phrases when somebody tapped lightly at my arm. I looked into Prentiss' face.

Headshrinker, I thought. Maybe that's what I need.

Prentiss turned away and I followed him to a neutral corner. Caroline Adams moved toward the stairs, looked back once, then went up and disappeared.

"Throwing you out?" Prentiss said.

"Looks as if," I said.

"Probably Jack Parrish's doing," he said.

I hadn't got around to thinking of Parrish. I had to admit the doctor was probably correct.

"Uh-huh," I said. "But what will I do? There isn't any other place in town."

He appeared to think about it.

"I could sleep in the car," I said. "But where would I brush my teeth?"

I had a bad reaction to the sound of my own voice. I happened to think about where Peter Davidian was brushing his teeth. I wondered whether he bothered any more.

"Excuse me," I said. "I'm all right. Let's get out in the fresh air."

There were the two suitcases and the smaller case containing my file on the Davidian matter. I had them in hand when I remembered my bill on the desk. I started over there, and Prentiss moved ahead of me to pick it up.

"I'll do it," he said. "Meet you outside."

He was turning into a fairly good guy.

I went outside, moving fast and not looking around. The two farmers had disappeared. The crowds on the street and sidewalks had dwindled quite a lot in the few minutes it had taken to check me out of the hotel. I walked to the corner and up the side street to where I had left my car. There was a U-drive behind it which no doubt would belong to Dr. Prentiss. He came along as I was throwing my bags into the back seat.

"There's a motel about halfway between Wesley and the county seat," he said. "Might do for a couple of days."

"Sure," I said, "and a couple of days is all we need, isn't it?"

He didn't say anything.

"Listen," I said, "Peter Davidian is holding out on us."

"Oh?" he said.

"He may be afraid to face up to his own—emotional disturbance, as you call it. Maybe he's afraid he really is crazy and he just can't admit it."

"Yes," Prentiss said. "Sam Birch and I talked about that before the interview today."

"That's why Sam kept after him."

"Yes."

"Maybe a new face, new voice, would get it out of him."

"Yours?" Prentiss said.

"May be worth a try," I said.

"I agree. When?"

"Well—tonight? Will they let me see him?"

"I'm sure Sam can set it up," he said.

"Can I fly back to Chicago with you, and I can pick up something for Stateville from there—"

"You can take me to Chicago, drop me, and keep the plane," he said.

"Then I guess that's what we'd better do. Eleven o'clock?"

"That's when the pilot expects me."

"I'll check in at the motel on the way."

"Fine," Prentiss said. "I'll see you at the plane. There's only one airport."

I nodded, walked around my car, got in, and got it started. It didn't take long to get out of town.

* * * *

The motel had at least one vacancy, which was all I needed. It was neither old nor new. Its only advantage over the hotel was that it had a bath for each unit. There was no telephone.

I paid for two nights, put my bags in the room, got out paper and a pen, and wrote a note to Miss Adams:

"Am at Shadyside Motel for a couple of days. Flying to the prison to-night to see Peter. Will return early morning. Please keep in touch. Mac."

There was a stamp machine in the motel office. I bought enough to make the postage plus special delivery, addressed the letter to Miss Caroline Adams at the Clark Hotel in Wesley, and dropped it in a box. Then I got back in the car and drove to the county seat, through it and two miles on into the country, and in that way I came to the airport.

Of three small planes on the open field, one was lighted up, and I walked about a quarter of a mile to reach it. The pilot was standing around smoking a cigarette, and inside I saw Dr. Prentiss, seated, reading some papers. I climbed in and sat across a narrow aisle from him. The pilot flipped his cigarette away, climbed in and closed the door, and took some time settling himself at the controls.

The plane was a comfortable twin-engine Beech, with three good seats. There had been six, but two on one side and one on the other had been removed, no doubt to make room for light cargo. The pilot was on the large side, but not so big as to overpower his small compartment. He stuck something up to his mouth and mumbled and I heard the static of the radio. Looking around, I couldn't see at first any control tower to which he might be talking. Then, far down the field to my left, lights blinked. The plane was shaking some under the strain of the brakes. The pilot gunned the engines briefly and it shook heavily, then eased off as he throttled down and released the brakes. We taxied slowly, curving onto a paved runway, then picked up speed and were heading into the blinking lights at the far end of the field when she lifted easily, banked southeasterly, and leveled off. Below on my left a small cluster of lights glimmered and dropped away fast. Wesley, I thought. Sleep tight.

I glanced at Dr. Prentiss, still engrossed in his reading, settled deep in the seat, and began consciously, muscle by muscle, to relax.

Dr. Prentiss read for about three minutes, made some marks on a manuscript, and put it away in his brief case.

"What do you think of our chances?" he said.

"About Peter? I have no idea. None. Working around that little town has been like trying to find a gray cat in a heavy fog."

"Do you think Miss Adams will be of any help to you?"

"Maybe. She has been some help. It took a while to break through to her."

"Does she have any commitment to Jack Parrish?"

"I don't think so. She may have a routine sense of loyalty. She's probably sympathetic about what happened to Esther. Also, she may be getting over the loyalty, after tonight."

He put his head back and closed his eyes. After a while he said:

"I suppose you feel we've put you on an elusive, improbable scent. At first we were going to try our own talents. One, maybe two of us at a time, asking questions around the town."

"Well, you would know what you were looking for anyway. I'm not even sure of that."

"We decided that a combination of bird-dog persistence and—uh—jungle cunning would be more useful on the job."

"I like that jungle cunning. What is that?"

He smiled a little. It was the first time and somewhat shocking.

"Excuse me, just a rough phrase. The thing is, ignorance can be helpful in some circumstances. The so-called experts can think so refined, they sometimes respond to insufficient suggestion. This wastes time."

He was losing me, but I appreciated the vote of confidence.

Jungle cunning, I thought. Not bad. I could put that on the door of my office in some way—"North Side Tiger—Your Prey Is My Meat."

Prentiss was serious again, leaning out into the aisle a little, speaking over the noise of the engines.

"You said Peter is holding out on us. How? In what area?"

I shrugged.

"Just a feeling," I said. "I doubt if it's fear of being thought crazy. I don't think he knows whether he's crazy or not, and I don't think he cares, at this point."

"You seemed to find some significance in his remark about Mary Carpenter—that she liked him."

"Yeah. You would not get that idea from talking to Mary Carpenter herself. The opposite you'd get."

"But that could be a cover too. She'd hardly admit to anyone that she had a fond feeling for a condemned murderer—the boy who killed her best friend."

"That best-friend business may not work out."

"I use the term to mean a status symbol. It would be very high-class in Wesley for Mary Carpenter to claim Esther Parrish for best friend."

"True. So they were friends in public. And each could do a service for the other."

He looked interested. I let him in on my theory, that Mary served as cover for some of Esther's shenanigans. In return, as Prentiss said, Esther gave Mary status. In that kind of a deal one or the other is likely to come up getting kicked in the teeth, and in this particular relationship the one most likely to get kicked was Mary.

"So," I said, "if Mary had a thing for Peter, she would resent being left to wait in the car on a cold day, especially if Esther went roaring off with Mary's boyfriend in the truck."

He nodded a couple of times.

"What kind of shenanigans do you think Esther was indulging in?" he asked.

"I'm not sure, and I'm not saying they were deadly serious or even very sensational. I have a hunch they involved older men. I don't know who. Fred Sampson still keeps a snapshot of Esther in a tin box in that old barn. Along with some ready cash."

His eyes moved jerkily.

"Fred Sampson?"

"If Fred Sampson was fooling around with Esther Parrish—and I admit it seems an unlikely pair—and if Peter knew it and if Peter had a thing going for Esther in spite of what he says now—and if he made some discovery about this that afternoon when he let Esther into the Sampson house to make coffee—that might make him feel 'goofy,' as he put it himself. He couldn't get back at Fred Sampson, for reasons he explained to Sam Birch. But he could attack Esther, if driven far enough."

He nodded some more.

"You're making sense," he said. "Keep going."

"That's as far as I can go. I can't explain why Peter would cover up a thing like that."

"For the same reason he couldn't fight Fred Sampson when the older man mistreated him," Prentiss said firmly.

"Maybe," I said. "In that case, maybe I can break him down."

He studied me carefully for about a minute.

"I hope so," he said. "I think you're on the right track." I wasn't sure of that at all, but it was nice of him to say so.

"Where would I have the best chance to find Sam," I asked, "to set up an interview with Peter?"

"Sam is probably home in bed," he said.

I nodded, put my head back, and closed my eyes. I was too keyed up to sleep, but I got in about ten minutes of forced relaxation before we came down in Chicago.

* * * *

At the airport the pilot agreed to stand by and Dr. Prentiss hung around while I got Sam on the telephone. He had been sound asleep, but he came alive all right when I made my pitch.

"I'll put in a call," he said. "It may take a while, middle of the night and all. But at a time like this the warden will lean over backward as far as he can. Stay where you are." I stayed in the phone booth and Dr. Prentiss paced the floor outside. We were in a far corner of a somewhat rundown terminal, and I kept smelling coffee but couldn't make out where they were selling it. I guess my nose twitched or something, because suddenly Prentiss disappeared. When he came back he had two paper cups of steaming coffee. We were working on it when the pilot strolled up with a paper cup of his own.

"You sleepy?" I asked.

"I'll be all right. I slept out there in the woods while I was waiting."

"Good," I said.

"It's all right," he said. "That machine can fly itself in a pinch."

"Yeah," I said.

We finished the coffee and got halfway through a refill before Sam called back.

"It's set," he said, "for two o'clock. Go to the warden's office. He'll be there too. Because of your status—or lack of it—he'll have to sit in. He said he wouldn't open his yap unless something pops."

"What could pop?"

"Well—in Peter's situation, you can figure a little nervousness, tension."

"I see. All right. Two o'clock."

"Is Dr. Prentiss still there?"

"Right here."

I put Prentiss on the phone and stood around with the pilot, drinking the coffee. Prentiss hung up and wished me luck.

"If you come up with anything that needs talking over," he said, "call Sam or me from the prison. We'll get the others out for a meeting. Sam's office. Any hour."

"You guys are really on this thing, huh?" I said.

"It means a great deal to all of us."

"Okay, do you want me to call either way?"

"Only if you have something we can help with. If you call from Stateville, there'll be time to have a car here for you. The warden will have you picked up at the plane down there."

"Then I guess I'm all set. When do you want to leave?" I asked the pilot.

He shrugged.

"Flight will take maybe forty-five minutes. It's only a quarter to one. I could use a sandwich."

"All right," I said. "Let's go."

Dr. Prentiss waved and walked off, not wasting any time, and the pilot and I found a snack bar adjoining a bar. I ordered a slug of bourbon and he ordered a cheeseburger and a glass of milk. He looked at my drink every once in a while, but as far as I know, he didn't sneak one in.

It took us a few minutes to get cleared from the control tower and we took off at one-ten. On this trip I managed to sleep a little, now and then.

CHAPTER 11

I rode in the back seat of a long black car toward the house where Peter Davidian lived. There were two men in the front seat and we didn't have any conversation because there was a double thickness of bulletproof glass between us. I supposed there was a speaking tube, but I didn't know how to activate it, and even if I had known, I wouldn't have been able to think of much to say.

All institutions look alike at night—squares of light at random with black, solid spaces between and around them. I had been here before, on legitimate business, but it had been long before, and I grew depressed in exact proportion to the speed of the car on the silent, deserted streets. We pulled up at a side entrance, which was a little eerie, but one of the two from the front seat came along with me, and making it to the warden's office was about the same as approaching the board room of a thriving corporation.

In the warden's private office there was a very big desk, covered with neat stacks of paper and file folders. The man who had brought me had checked out my credentials at the plane, but the warden wanted a look too. I laid my I.D stuff on the desk and he looked at it for a few seconds, then nodded and let me pick it up. He was friendly enough after that. He offered me a big, comfortable chair, which I accepted, a cigar, which I declined, and then he leaned back in a somewhat squeaky swivel chair and pressed a button. While we waited for Peter Davidian to be brought in, he dismissed the man who had brought me. The two of us had the room to ourselves for a few minutes.

"Any chance for this kid?" he asked.

"Not much," I said. "I'm working out of desperation."

He shook his head.

"How is he as a guest?" I asked.

"No problem," he said.

"Is that good or bad?"

He seemed to think about it.

"Both good and bad. It saves a little trouble. On the other hand, I hate to see a kid like that give up. I know a man is supposed to accept his end and get resigned to it and all that, but I hate to see it."

"You think Peter has given up?"

"I think so," he said.

"Easier maybe," I said.

"I guess so. But I hate to see it."

There was a clicking sound and the warden pressed another button. The office door swung open to my left, and a guard came in with Peter Davidian.

"You can wait outside, Harry," the warden said.

The guard backed out and closed the door.

"Sorry to get you out so late, Peter," the warden said. "I guess you've had plenty of conversation today, huh?"

"It's all right," Peter said dully.

He was about six feet tall, slim without being skinny, and well made around the shoulders. He had big hands that hung straight out of his colorless prison shirt, and very large feet. He had stiff black hair, brushed back. It had been trimmed lately and not too well, and he was pale around the ears. He wouldn't have been a bad-looking kid if it hadn't been for those eyes. Not only were they so badly crossed that his pupils seemed to be hung on the bridge of his nose, but they were also narrow, and the left was narrower than the right, so that he appeared to be looking out between the slits of a homemade Halloween mask. There was no use trying to get a direct look from him. He wasn't able to make it mechanically.

The warden introduced me and Peter appeared to glance at me. I couldn't be sure.

"Hello," he said.

"Hello, Peter. I'm working for Sam Birch."

He shrugged lightly.

"Would you like some coffee, anything to drink?" the warden asked.

"No—thanks," Peter said. "Coffee keeps me awake."

When they're putting you down for the last time, I thought, they do it real nice.

"All right," the warden said, "you go ahead and talk to the visitor. No sweat."

He nodded to me, swung slowly in his big chair, put his back to the desk and the room, propped up his feet, and opened a book.

"Sit down, Peter," I said. "As Mr. O'Brien said, no sweat. I'd like to go over some things with you."

After a pause he sat down on the edge of a leather chair, drapped his big hands over his knees, and stared at the floor.

"I already talked to Mr. Birch quite a lot," he said.

"I know, and he told me about it. But there are some points I keep thinking about, I'd like to get my own slant on. For instance, if you'll try to remember back to that afternoon when you fixed the tire for Esther—"

His face twisted violently and his head jerked, as if he had been struck behind the ear. I could feel the pain in him as if it were my own.

"I know it's tough," I said, "but I wish you'd try. Try to remember your thoughts and feelings, minute by minute. When the jack broke down on you out there on the road, and you were going to drive home to get another one, Esther decided to go with you and leave Mary with the car. How did Mary react to that?"

"What—react? I don't—"

"Did she put up an argument? It was a cold day to sit around waiting…"

"No, she didn't argue. She just said, 'Okay, I'll wait.'"

"Well, how did you feel about it? Did you feel Esther ought to have asked Mary to go along with you in the truck?"

He shrugged.

"I didn't think much about it."

"Were you glad to be alone with Esther in the truck?"

"Me? No—I didn't care one way or the other. She said she wanted to go—"

"Did Esther tease you when you were alone with her?"

"You mean that day?"

"Any time. Did she tease you when you were alone with her, or only when there was somebody else around?"

"I don't know—I wasn't hardly ever alone with her."

"So she didn't tease you while you were driving the truck home to pick up a jack. What did you talk about? Do you remember?"

"No, I wouldn't remember—just anything, the weather, the flat tire—"

"Was she nervous or upset about anything?"

"No, I don't think—she was always kind of nervous, fidgety."

"Were you nervous? You'd spent all that time trying to help her and it was getting late. Did you want to get away from her?"

"Yeah, sort of, I guess. I guess so. She made me nervous sometimes."

"Can you think of some other times she made you nervous?"

The stiff hair on his scalp shifted as his forehead grew deep lines.

"Most of the time—school, around the place—she made me nervous."

"How would it make you feel inside? Did you get sore about it? Bugged?"

"Well…I—sometimes—"

"Would you get sore the way you did when you went after that cow with a pitchfork?"

Without warning, he smacked his right fist against his left palm. The warden's chair squeaked slightly. I had touched some nerve.

"No! I wouldn't do that—I mean, I wasn't sore at the cow—"

"What were you sore at? Fred Sampson?"

"No! Listen, Fred Sampson was like a father to me! People keep asking me about that—"

"People like Sam Birch, you mean?"

"Yeah—and everybody!"

I waited till the atmosphere stopped crackling.

"Did you know," I asked him finally, "that Fred Sampson kept a photograph of Esther Parrish in a strongbox in that old barn?"

There was a long silence. He sat with his face turned down, his big hands limp on his knees, his shoulders sagging forward.

"Yeah—I knew it," he said quietly. "I saw it once."

"When? When did you first see the picture?"

This is important, I thought. Stay with me, Peter!

"Oh," he said, "not too long—I mean, around then—"

"Was it that same day, the day you fixed the tire for Esther?"

"No—before—I lost—I mean—"

"It was your picture first, is that it?"

"No, I didn't mean—"

"And Fred Sampson found it and kept it?"

"Well, I don't know—if he just found it someplace—"

"Why would he keep it?"

"I don't know!"

He had begun tapping his feet on the floor, alternating them irregularly. I let things cool down again.

"Did you find it in Fred's strongbox?"

"I—yeah—I knew about the box."

"When you found it in there, why didn't you steal it back?"

"Steal! It didn't mean anything to me."

"Did Esther give it to you?"

"No. Mary gave it to me."

"Mary Carpenter gave it to you?"

"Yeah."

"Like kind of a joke, was it?"

"Uh-huh. It was kind of a joke."

"You told Sam Birch that Mary kind of liked you."

"I guess so."

"But you didn't care about her much?"

He shrugged.

"She's—funny—I never cared about—"

"All right, let's get away from girls for a while. Let's talk about some men around town."

"I didn't know too many…"

"You must have known a few. You had to go into town, Saturdays, buy things. Like the day before the flat-tire business, you drove into Jack Parrish's garage and warned a couple of mechanics that something might happen to Esther."

"I—what—?"

I looked at him. He was looking in my direction with those deep lines in his forehead.

"You drove in to Jack Parrish's place and told Tony Bledsoe something would happen to Esther if Jack didn't watch out."

"When?"

"The day before."

"How would I do that? I never did anything like that."

"You didn't? For sure?"

"I swear to God I never did that. Anyway, if I was going to do anything like that, I wouldn't tell Tony Bledsoe."

"Why not?"

"Well—we didn't get along. He didn't like me."

"Did he pick on you?"

"Yeah—I guess you could call it that."

"Tony kind of picks on everybody, doesn't he? Kind of a bully?"

"Everybody except Mr. Parrish, I guess."

"You acquainted with one of the other mechanics at Jack Parrish's—a fellow named Bud?"

"Bud Carney. Sure, I know him. He's all right."

"Who else? Chris Duval?"

"Yeah, Chris—he's nutty. Feeble-minded."

"Got a great memory."

"I know it."

"Anybody else you can think of—guys around town you got along with all right?"

"Well, there was lots of guys I got along with all right. What do you…?"

"Okay, let's get to something else."

Suddenly he stood up.

"I don't want to talk about it any more," he said.

He had said it firmly and quietly. I felt as if someone were holding a glass of water one inch from my mouth, just out of reach, and I was dying of thirst.

"Listen, Peter—" I said.

The warden's chair squeaked.

"No more," Peter said. "I talked and talked—it's no use. I know all those men—doctors, psychologists, whatever they are—they're trying to help me. I don't want it! Hear? It's no use!"

"All right—" I said.

"For the last time," he said. "I did it. I killed her, hear? I let her in the house out there; she said she wanted some coffee. I showed her the stuff, where it was, and she started to make coffee. So I said I'd go change the tire and bring the car back, and she said not to go yet, have some coffee and we would have some fun first. Play house, she said.

"So I stayed awhile and she made the coffee and we drank some. She kept looking at her watch. I didn't know—she was making me feel funny, nervous, goofy. So pretty soon we were in the parlor, in the front of the house, and she was—kind of monkeying around—I didn't know what to think. She was a real pretty girl, you know, and I never thought she cared about me. And so we were monkeying around on the sofa in the parlor and I heard somebody come up on the porch. And I started to get up and she grabbed me and wouldn't let me. Then I told her there was somebody out there, and she got scared and pushed me away. She told me not to go to the door but go out the back and she would wait in the house and I could pick her up when the car was fixed. She had me so mixed up I just did what she told me. Somebody was knocking on the front door, but I didn't go to it. I just went out the back and got in the truck. When I drove out to the road, there wasn't any car around and I didn't see anybody on the porch or walking around.

"Then I drove to where the car was and changed the tire. Mary was gone. I drove Esther's car back to the house. When I went in, she was lying on the sofa, asleep. I started monkeying around and she woke up and started fighting me. I was really goofy by then. I hit her in the head and she fainted or something. Then I was scared. I carried her out to the car and went back to the house and got the knife. I don't know why I got the knife. I wasn't thinkin'—see—I drove to the old barn and took her in there and tried to bring her around, but I couldn't. I was going to take her in town to a doctor, but then I was too scared to do that. I left her there and walked across the field to the truck and drove into town. I didn't know what to do. I just sat there and stewed. Finally I drove back to the barn, hid the truck up the road, and went in. She was still there, lying there. I don't know what happened—I mean, I was goofy—I had the knife in my hand. And then the next thing I knew, they started coming in. Tony Bledsoe—I remember him—he started for me and I ducked into one of the stalls. Then there was police, sheriffs—and Mr. Parrish was there and they had to hold him—and that's what happened."

His hands were shaking. The warden had half-turned in his chair and was sitting with his right hand on the desk, near his buttons. I knew the talking was over for that night. I nodded.

"Listen…" Peter was saying. "I did it. I admitted it—all along. I'll take what's comin' to me. I only wish it was right now. You tell those men, those doctors—I don't want help. For what I did, I got it comin'. And that's all."

"All right, Peter," the warden said. "Thanks for telling us."

He pressed a button, the door opened, and the guard came in. When he touched Peter's arm, the boy turned and went out, not looking back.

I got on my feet.

"Sorry," the warden said. "I'll call your car."

I couldn't think of anything to say. I was preoccupied. I must have sat there about two minutes before the door opened and the chauffeur looked in. I said good night to the warden and went out in much the same way Peter had gone out with the guard.

Sitting behind the bulletproof glass in the big car, I nursed my preoc-cupation. There was only one in the front seat this time. I was glad the other could be getting some rest.

The pilot was resting on the floor of the plane, curled up on some spread-out newspapers. I woke him and asked for directions to a phone. He came out of his sleep reluctantly and pointed out the dim light of a phone booth about a block away. I left him to warm up his engines and walked down there. I had two telephone numbers, one for Dr. Prentiss and one for Sam Birch. I flipped the dime, heads for Prentiss, tails for Sam, and it came up heads.

Good, I thought. Sam can get some sleep.

I waited a couple of minutes and Prentiss came on.

"You talked to Peter?" he asked.

"Yeah—yeah, I did."

"What do you think?"

"I've got a lot of thoughts to sort out. One thing I'm thinking is that a lot of time has run down the gutters."

"I guess I'm not with you," he said.

"You guys are in this for yourselves, not for Peter."

"I beg your pardon?"

"I know it would be a big deal for you to get the kid off, make a fine point, large step forward in psycho-legal justice, or whatever you call it. But this is a good way to lose sight of the main idea—which is Peter Davidian."

"Of course…"

"See if I'm right. The only way you would be able to straighten him out—if he gets off—is by removing his sense of guilt about the killing. That right?"

"That's a large chunk of it. It would take time."

"He needs that guilt."

"Well—I don't—"

"He is so full of it, the electric chair is his only out! Tonight he fired you—all of you. He is ready to die, to pay for what he did. He doesn't want you. He doesn't need you."

"I'm sure he could—"

"Funny thing is, he doesn't know it yet, but he really doesn't need you—anyway, not the way you've been trying to help. He didn't do it."

There was a pause.

"What did you say?" Prentiss said finally.

"He didn't do it. He didn't kill Esther Parrish."

"You can prove this?"

"Not tonight. I didn't tell the warden. I didn't even tell Peter. Partly because I didn't figure it out soon enough. And I didn't want to raise any false hopes. I might fall on my face. I might not be able to get proof in time. But I'm going to give it a try."

"Well—I'm astonished! Good luck."

"You can help me this way. Call Sam Birch and tell him Peter didn't do it. Tell him to hang on the phone. I'll call when I can."

"Yes, of course. Right away. You're going—?"

"Back to Wesley," I said. "Good night, Doctor."

I hung up and walked back to the plane. The engines were idling and the pilot stood outside, smoking.

"Ready?" he said.

"Back to the woods," I said, "if you have the time."

"If you've got the money."

"You can be sure of getting it."

"Then let's go."

I climbed the wing, got into the cabin and into my seat. The take-off was smooth and easy, and I was asleep before the prison lights could have faded from view.

CHAPTER 12

In the motel room I slept for about two hours and woke to the buzzing of insects and a knocking at my door. When I opened it the manager was outside, wearing a bathrobe. He wasn't cordial.

"Phone call," he said.

"Where will I take it?"

He stabbed with his thumb over his shoulder.

"Be right down," I said, and closed the door.

I pulled on some pants, put on a jacket, and when I went outside, he was still waiting. We walked toward the office where a telephone booth stood in an alcove.

"You were stayin' at the Clark House in Wesley?" he asked.

"Right," I said.

"I'll have to ask you to move."

"Why?"

"No matter why. Just check out."

I stopped at the booth and gave him a look and he looked around here and there. His mouth was firm, however, and I knew he meant what he said.

"Be all right if I take my call first?" I said.

He shrugged.

"Go ahead. But don't be too long."

The phone call was from Caroline Adams.

"Your letter just came," she said. "Are you all right?"

"I'm fine. I just got thrown out of another place."

"Oh no!"

"It's all right. How are you?"

"I—don't know. I didn't get much sleep."

"Hear anything from Mr. Parrish?"

"No."

"I had a talk with Peter Davidian earlier this morning."

"You went all the way to the—prison?"

"Yes. Didn't take long. Very interesting talk."

"What happened?"

"It would take a long time to go into it now. Are you up for all day?"

"Yes, of course."

"How about some breakfast?"

"Well—"

"If you'll drive this far, I'll meet you and we'll go on. The only reason I don't drive into town for you is that I'm unwelcome around there and I don't want any of it to rub off on you."

"All right. In about half an hour?"

"I'll be here."

As I left the booth, the manager looked out of the office.

"I'm on my way," I said. "Have no fears."

He went back inside and closed the door.

In my room I repacked my bags, making sure the file on the Peter Davidian case was intact. Whoever had packed for me, preparatory to throwing me out, had been a little sloppy. The file evidently hadn't been touched. Not much wonder there. Parrish wasn't interested in the file. He had it made. All he had to do was to get rid of me.

I stalled around for about fifteen minutes, then left the room and put the bags in the car. I went to the office to return my key and the manager was not in sight. It figured.

A hundred yards down the road toward the county seat there was a grove of trees and a turnout. I left the motel, drove down there, turned around, and stopped in the trees at a point from which I could watch the motel entrance.

After five or six minutes a green Chevrolet sedan turned into the motel drive, slid to a stop, and let out two fellows. One was big and one was little and scrawny. The big one was Tony Bledsoe. I wondered how the little mechanic enjoyed being dragged out early Sunday morning to run errands for the boss.

The two of them went into the office. I counted to three; they came out, got into the car, and drove away, back toward Wesley.

Operation he's got, I thought. He's been reading books.

I settled back in the seat and waited for Caroline Adams.

I waited quite awhile. It was ten minutes after nine when I saw her approaching, not too fast, not too slow. She hesitated at the motel drive and I pulled out from the trees, swung down in her direction, and stopped across from her on the road.

"Good morning," she said.

"Hi," I said. "You know where we can get some breakfast?"

"I think there's a place open today—it will take a few minutes."

"You lead," I said. "Don't drive too fast."

She smiled, somewhat tentatively, and got going. I made a U-turn on the highway and traveled in her wake.

* * * *

On the far outskirts of the county seat there was a roadside coffee shop. She turned in there and parked and I pulled in beside her. Following her, I had learned how hungry I was. I hadn't eaten, now that I thought of it, since dinner the night before. I had not had very much sleep, and the muscles of my neck and head were tight as guitar strings. Also, I was nervous. Somebody slammed a car door some distance away and I jumped as I opened her door and let her out.

Inside the aromas were warm and friendly. We found a table at a window and sunshine fell across the typewritten menu.

"Well," she said, "what next? I never saw anyone get thrown out of a hotel before. I must say, you took it coolly."

"External impression," I said. "I wasn't cool on the inside."

"Who is?" she said.

We ordered, got some coffee served, and after we'd had a couple of sips it became possible to talk.

"You said you talked to Peter," she said. "What did he say?"

"He said quite a lot. Very interesting."

She fooled around with the coffee-cup handle.

"What are you going to do?" she asked.

"First I am going to have a good breakfast. Then I am going to try to find another place to stow my hat, a check-in point. Then I am going hunting."

"What are you hunting? What kind of game?"

"Killer game. The person who killed Esther Parrish."

She was pretty cool herself. She didn't betray surprise, but on the other hand, she didn't shrug. She was listening.

"Peter didn't do it," I said. "I'm positive of it."

"Then what's to do?" she said. "Can't you just tell them he didn't do it and explain how you know and they'll start looking for the one who really did?"

The waitress came with a couple of plates of bacon and eggs and rolls and so on, and we waited while she set them down.

"That won't work," I said. "If there were more time, maybe. But there's only till eight o'clock tomorrow morning."

She winced, closed her eyes, and opened them slowly. "Who did it?" she asked.

I had a mouthful of hot scrambled eggs and had to apologize with gestures. She let it go. When my mouth cleared I said:

"Even if I positively knew and had him in hand, I wouldn't tell you right now. That kind of knowledge is heavy to carry around."

She made an impatient gesture.

"You're playing some kind of game with me," she said. "I don't understand it. Eat your breakfast."

"Okay."

I didn't say any more till we had got through all the bacon, eggs, and rolls and were on the third cup of coffee. She didn't say anything either. Then, after some finicky business with her napkin, vanity, and something under the table that looked as if she were straightening her stockings, she leaned forward with both fists against the edge of the table and she said:

"All right! I'm a schoolteacher, not a detective. I've lived in this town for three years. I know everybody in town. The murder of Esther Parrish was a horrible, disgusting, frightening, bad thing. What do you want from me? What did you expect?"

So she had come around. I smiled and she hung there on the edge of the table, waiting.

"Now you're leveling," I said. "I don't think I really know what I want, and you've given me a lot more help than I had any right to expect. So much for that. What I have to do is to talk, real straight, with Mary Carpenter, Chris Duval, the town constable, and eventually a few others maybe. I have to manage to do it quietly so that no big shuffle will develop, in which the large target might disappear. Because the only way I can save Peter Davidian's life is to produce his stand-in. You can help me. But I understand your situation and I'm not asking."

She gazed at me. I couldn't read anything in her face. I had just given up trying when she moved her right hand lazily from the table and slapped me in the face, very smartly. Somewhere in the restaurant somebody dropped a knife, or spoon, or fork on the floor.

"You've been asking for that," she said. "Now go ahead and lay it on the line for me."

I resisted the temptation to massage my face.

She'll be all right, I thought.

"When we leave here," I said, "I'll go look up Chris Duval. If I'm lucky, he'll be at home. While I'm doing that, you can line up Mary Carpenter for me. The best way to talk to her would be away from her own home, maybe in some place like this. Is the Glade open on Sundays?"

"I'll find out," she said.

"How can I check in with you?"

"At the hotel."

"Good. Now let me give you some background."

"Please," she said. "And say it simple so I can understand."

"Peter isn't crazy," I said. "I'm sure he wasn't crazy on that fatal day. But he's mixed up. It doesn't take a psychologist to know that memory plays tricks on people. When they're under acute stress it plays very odd tricks. It played tricks on Peter Davidian. For one thing, people kept telling him he killed Esther Parrish, and finally he got so he believed it. In order to believe it, he had to construct a system in which he could have done it. That is what he did. He had plenty of time to work on it, and he tried it different ways and finally he got it almost perfect. He tried it on me early this morning and it was a beautiful invention. The only thing wrong with it was that a couple of the things he claimed to have done were impossible. I knew otherwise, from what I had already dug up. One of the most deceitful tricks the memory plays on people has to do with sequence, timing. Peter had to work very hard to make the timing work out. Gaps kept showing up. And finally he filled in the gaps with what he imagined he must have done. The ironic thing is that the people who were working the hardest to save him encouraged him to go ahead and make the invention. And the better the story got, the more they went along with it."

I stopped. She had her chin propped on her two hands and her eyes were fixed on my mouth.

"That simple enough?" I asked.

"I guess so," she said. "I believe you."

"I'm glad. Then we'd better get started. If you can line Mary up for a talk, I'll get myself a room somewhere and try to get Chris Duval to turn his mouth on. I'll call you at the hotel, all right?"

"Yes, all right."

I left money for the tab and we started out. At the door I took her arm.

"This is risky business for you," I said. "Slap me again if you have to, but I want to be sure you feel all right about it."

She looked at me very steady out of clear blue eyes.

"I feel just fine about it," she said.

I nodded and helped her into her car.

"I take your word for it," I said. "I'll be calling you."

She didn't say anything. She was busy getting the car started and pulling away.

Hang in, I thought on her behalf. Hang in strong. It may get rough.

Downtown in the county seat there was a good-sized hotel. I decided Jack Parrish's influence didn't extend this far because they didn't hesitate to give me a room. It wasn't much newer than the rooms at the Clark in

Wesley but it was bigger and it had a bath and telephone. I made sure the telephone worked by placing a call to Sam Birch. It went through quickly. Sam's voice was hoarse from lack of sleep and husky with tension.

"You ought to keep in touch," he said. "I haven't heard anything since Prentiss called me at four in the morning. What's going on? You put him down, I hear."

"Not just him. I didn't mean to put him down. I can't go into the details now, but I'm on the case. I wanted to be sure I could reach you."

"It's eight tomorrow morning for sure," he said, "unless you come up with something. I got turned down on a stay by every justice in Washington. There's nowhere else to go."

"I know what time it is," I said. "One thing you might try—talk to that warden, O'Brien, and tell him we've got something good working and if he can stall around any it would be mighty friendly of him. He can't do it, but he might if you push him."

"I'll try it. I don't think he'll stall."

"Okay. What do you have to have for the governor, specifically?"

"I only have to be able to say, 'We've got positive new evidence in the Davidian case.' If it turns out I'm making it up, they just go ahead and turn on the juice a few hours later. Then I would eventually get disbarred and that would be all."

"All right," I said, "you're too good a lawyer to get disbarred. I'll call you. How can I always reach you?"

He gave me a number, different from the one I had just called.

"The answering service will keep it open for me," he said.

I wrote it down.

"Good," I said. "All you got to do is lie around and watch the football game and read the paper and have a few snorts. If you think of it, you might keep your fingers crossed."

"If I think of it," he said. "Goodbye, Mac."

It was eleven o'clock when I left the hotel. I drove to the edge of town and a mile beyond and stopped on the road.

With feeling up the way it is, I thought, it's not smart to drive this familiar-looking car around the neighborhood.

I made a U-turn, drove back into town, and found the U-drive place where Prentiss had got his car the night before. I arranged for a new Detroit-style powerhouse and waited while they put my own car away out of sight. Then I got started again and drove to the gray-brown shack on the edge of town where Chris Duval lived.

He took better care of the hotel and stores, I decided, than he did of his own place. Weeds grew thick in the small front yard, and the brown picket fence surrounding it was overgrown with tangled creepers, dry and untended. The screen door rattled when I knocked. There was no response, and I knocked again in vain and found my way by a dirt path to the rear of the house. Chris, stripped to the waist, was drawing water from a pump under a rickety overhang outside the kitchen. He jumped like a rabbit when my shadow fell across the runoff trough under the pump.

"Take it easy, Chris. It's only me," I said. "How are you?"

No answer. He got busy with his pan of water, spilled a little of it, scurried away into the kitchen to get rid of it, then came back and peered at me from the doorway.

"I was thinking about what you told me," I said, "about the day Esther Parrish was killed."

If he remembered that he hadn't told me anything at all, I was dead. But that was the kind of thing he might get mixed up on. Outside facts he remembered. Inside facts might elude him.

"Esther Parrish got killed," he said. "Pretty girl. Too bad."

"Yes, it was. You were working that night when they found her. At the hotel, wasn't it?"

"Workin' at the hotel, cleanin' up. Folks sitting around talking about the posse—Mr. Parrish got up a posse."

"But you were working in the hotel lobby."

"In the lobby," he said. "Lots of folks there. I remember them. Saul Wright was talkin' to Jess. George Medford in the corner was talkin' to Bud White, old Bud, that is—sixty-eight years old, born on April seventh—"

My clenched fists were holding sweat.

"Yeah," I said. "And there were others there too?"

"Sure, big crowd that night. Frank Judson sittin' there readin' the newspaper like nothin' happened. Tony Bledsoe talkin' about bein' too late to join the posse, frettin' all the time—"

He stared out of his bright little eyes and turned and disappeared in the kitchen. I waited, opening and closing my stiff hands. When he came back, he had a shirt on.

"You got to go now," he said. "I got to go to work."

"Okay," I said. "Want a ride downtown?"

"No—no ride. I always walk."

He darted out of the kitchen, skirted me warily, and headed toward the front of the house by the dirt path. He was talking to himself now.

"Esther Parrish—pretty girl—too bad."

I had got what he had for that day. Maybe it would be enough.

The main street, from the hotel to the town hall, looked like a ghost town. Nobody in sight. No cars parked at the curb. A solitary man in work clothes rumbled past me in a pickup as I turned the corner and drifted to a stop under a tree. I left the car to the sound of church bells. Up the street, a block beyond the hotel, was a gas station. I walked up there, not too fast. It was warm in the sun and cool in the shade. I passed from one to the other and back again.

There was a coin telephone on the outside wall of the station. I put a dime in it and dialed the hotel number. Old Jess came on. I asked to speak to Miss Adams.

"Don't know if she's in," he said.

"Could you find out?"

"Reckon I could. Can I say who's callin'?"

"Just a friend from out of town," I said.

"Hang on."

I hung on for what seemed like an hour. Then Caroline Adams came on.

"It's me," I said.

"Listen, I haven't been able to talk to Mary yet," she said. "She went to church with her mother. I'll just have to keep trying."

"All right."

"How are you coming?"

"Okay so far, but the clock is bugging me. I've got decisions to make. Have you seen Jack Parrish around anywhere?"

"No. He called me, here, before I got back—you know. I haven't returned the call."

"Maybe you should."

"Where are you?"

"Up the street. I don't want to hang around much till I get some things wrapped up. I don't want to get caught in that possible shuffle."

"Where will you go?"

"I don't know. I'll drive around. I'll call you in maybe twenty minutes."

"All right. I'll stay in the lobby. That may make it simpler."

"Whatever you think. Goodbye for now."

"Yes."

I hung up and left the booth. Inside the station shack the attendant was propped on his elbows over a littered desk, reading the Sunday paper. I left him in peace to enjoy it.

Returning toward where I had left the car, I started across the street halfway up the block, moving on a long diagonal. I walked slowly, reluctant to get back to gasoline and pistons. It was a very nice day. On the far side of the street trees were set in a formal row. They were old, well-established trees, high and spreading, and threw leaf patterns against the sun on the pavement. No cars passed to interrupt the faintly fluttering shadows. Ahead, where the main four corners of town intersected, there were no trees, only bright sunlight, clear and unshadowed.

Then suddenly, in a way I had no chance to anticipate, there was a shadow. It moved, bulky and deliberate, from nowhere into the exact center of the four corners, below the suspended traffic signal that flashed at intervals vainly, without purpose. It was a man, not a shadow. It was Jack Parrish, in slacks and a sport shirt. And a gun. He had this gun under his arm, long-barreled, high-powered. He stopped in the middle of the big intersection as I stopped in the middle of the side street, fifty yards away from him.

There was nothing about it, for a few seconds, real enough to respond to.

I'm dreaming, I thought. This situation has never really occurred in the twentieth century. It died out, it went away. Any second now, if I see what I think I see, there will be a siren and a couple of well-trained officers will take over the wild man in the middle of the public street.

But then there wasn't any siren and just the two of us—and we knew each other, no doubt about that—and it became real. There wasn't any logical reason for it not to be real. It was just that it was the kind of thing that doesn't actually happen.

Nothing illogical about that, I thought.

It was awfully quiet. Somewhere in the background, far from the two of us, there were sounds, dull voices, cars starting, stopping. There would be churches back there, up in the town, and people would be coming and going. There wouldn't be much reason for any of them to come down these main streets early Sunday afternoon, what with the stores closed and all.

Parrish was just standing there, the gun hanging in his arm loop.

"Watch it," I said, not raising my voice.

He didn't say anything. I took a couple of steps, and he lifted the barrel and got the end of it on me. Not that I could pinpoint it with my naked eyes, but there are those guesses you make and those you shy away from making, both negative and positive.

It occurred to me that the way things had been going around this town for several months, Jack Parrish just might be able to knock me out for good and get away with it. At about the same moment it occurred to me that the clock hadn't stopped and I didn't have time to hang around and wait to see what might happen. The thing to do was to get away from that gun, into the car and away, and figure things out while moving.

A funny thing was, I wasn't scared. I had been scared many times facing a loaded gun in an unpredictable hand, but now, maybe because I didn't really believe he would use it, maybe because I was fascinated by the scene, I couldn't be scared. It was a pity, because if I had been more scared, I would have been more alert and everything would have gone much more pleasantly.

My rented car was about twenty-five feet away, on a slant, from my left shoulder. I tried to remember whether I had locked it. I thought not, but I wasn't sure. I put my hand in my pocket, and Parrish stood like a statue with the gun. I got the slim coupling of keys in my fist, counted to three and moved forward, ducking, side-stepping once, then rolling onto my shoulder and back on the street. I kept on rolling over and over, scrambling with my toes and fingers, toward the big car. No shot sounded from Parrish's gun. I rolled from sunlight into shadow and came up against the left front wheel of the car, slithered out from under the bumper and pushed up to my knees to look down toward the four corners.

Parrish had disappeared. I waited long enough to make sure he was no longer standing there under the traffic light, then pushed up onto my feet and moved, somewhat hunched with pain and anxiety, to the car door on the curb side. Two men rose from a crouch to greet me. One was Tony Bledsoe; the other was the lanky mechanic named Bud. Bud Carney, somebody had called him.

I started to back off and a third one showed up behind me off the left. He could have come from the alley six steps away. He kicked the back of my left knee and my leg went out. I fell sideways against the front fender. When I tried to push away from it, Tony Bledsoe, the biggest one, had both arms around my neck from behind, pulling up, and the one named Bud was digging the car keys out of my fist.

"Get the keys and let's go," Bledsoe said.

He hung onto my neck while somebody got the car door open in back. Then he gave me a boot at the end of my spine and half pushed, half dragged me to the opening. The third one, the little mechanic, as it turned out, came along beside us, doing an odd kind of jig.

It was the kind of thing you don't fight at the time because you can't get anything working. I was neither on my feet nor my knees. My hands and arms were useless because there was nothing to take hold of. The pressure on my neck and back was crucial and incapacitating. I only wanted to save the vertebrae from destruction.

"You drive," Bledsoe said, as I looked into the open back seat. "Get in," he said.

The little mechanic hopped into the seat and bounced to the far side.

"Now you," Bledsoe said.

He hung onto my neck till he could bend my head and shoulders into the opening. Then, using his foot again low on my back, he shoved me forward. I went along with it, for fear he might slam the door on my feet. I felt the lurch as he swung onto the seat, heard the car door slam and the engine rumble softly. Then we were moving. I was glad I had rented the big car. The ride could have been rougher.

It was rough enough. I had banged my head rolling across the pavement and the lumps were throbbing badly. My neck had been twisted hard and my throat ached. One of my eyes was swollen shut. I couldn't remember when it had been hit. I lay still, stretched in the middle and curled at the ends, racked over the slight hump that divided the seat, thankful that the floor was carpeted. It took a long time to get my breathing smoothed out. When I moved a little, experimentally, Bledsoe put his foot on my hip.

"Lie still and take it easy," he said.

We were traveling fast without speeding and I assumed we had left the town behind. There was a smell of hay and clover in the air. It's a nice fragrance, but it didn't soothe me now. Way back in that mental place where it hurts the most I was getting sick. I had underestimated Parrish's drive and Bledsoe's rough-and-ready know-how. He was an amateur, but he was a good, strong amateur. It had been foolish of me to drive downtown to call Caroline Adams. I could have done it from some distance. But I hadn't figured on Parrish. And as a result, if I guessed right, I would be helpless somewhere until after eight o'clock Monday morning, and that was all they cared about.

I hope you have a good dream or two, Peter, I thought. That's what you've got left.

It wasn't possible this had been done to me. But it had been done. I put my cheek against the carpet and gave in to the motion of the car. The sickness squirmed in me like a dying snake.

CHAPTER 13

We turned left, not too fast, then a few seconds later left again, very sharp. My head rammed up against the door. Luckily, since it was an expensive car, there was some padding, but it didn't help my twisted neck. The ride wasn't smooth any more. It was rough and uncertain, as if there weren't any road at all.

But it didn't last long. The car stopped and Bledsoe's big feet scraped over me. One of them banged my kneecap as he got the door open and left the car. I moved my head back suddenly as the little mechanic opened the door on his side. He caught me in the clavicle, but his feet were smaller and it wasn't so rough.

The door at my feet slammed shut, and a moment later Bledsoe was leaning into the car over my face.

"Come on, get out," he said.

The engine was still rumbling. Looking up, I saw the tall one, Bud, in the front seat, his neck twisted as he looked back and down. I couldn't see his eyes.

I got up on my knees, got a hand on the back seat, and pushed myself halfway out of the car.

"I'll get out," I said. "Can I say something?"

"If you can talk while you're moving," Bledsoe said.

Speaking up so the one named Bud could certainly hear, I said:

"You're going to a lot of useless effort. I talked to Davidian's lawyer this morning. He's given up. The governor turned down the last appeal. The warden has told Davidian there's no more hope."

Bledsoe's bruised, lumpy face turned for a moment toward Bud's. He had a big wrist watch on one hairy arm and he had a look at it.

"That's good," he said. "Nothing to worry about. We just sit around and have a long, quiet Sunday. You can get out now."

I straightened up some more, got a foot out, leaned on it, and got the other one out. Bledsoe pushed me clear of the door and slammed it shut. The little mechanic was standing around on one and a half feet. I would have tried something against the odds of the two of them, but I wasn't sure of Bud, and with three of them I wouldn't have a chance. With time a chance might turn up.

Time, I thought. Lots of time.

"Get the car out of here," Bledsoe was saying to Bud. "You know where mine is. Report in. Then bring back some coffee and sandwiches. Get some beer too. Might as well be comfortable. Be a long wait."

"Okay," Bud said.

I had one more oral shot at it.

"Kidnapping," I said. "Very rough rap."

"Yeah," Bledsoe said. "Hold it, Bud. You—turn around."

"Me?" I said.

"Come on—"

The small mechanic moved nervously. I turned around, facing the car. Bledsoe pushed at the small of my back and I bumped my nose against the hard edge of the drain trough on the car top. There was the musty odor of dry seed, the soft stench of decay from the old barnyard. Bledsoe grabbed my wrists and pulled them back. I heard the clink of metal, felt the cold bite of steel as he slapped handcuffs on me.

"Be sure not to lose the key," the little mechanic said, and giggled.

It had been the first word out of him. I wondered how it felt to live where he did inside his head.

Bledsoe gave a yank on my linked wrists and I backed off from the car.

"Get going," Bledsoe said.

Bud gunned the motor. He swung into a wide turn over the barnyard, straightened out, and went past us, throwing dust, into the lane toward the road. Bledsoe nudged at my shoulder, turning me.

"In the barn," he said. "Out of the sun."

I walked awkwardly against the pull of my manacled wrists toward the abandoned barn where Esther Parrish had been murdered. But I wasn't thinking about Esther Parrish. I was thinking about Caroline Adams sitting around the hotel lobby, waiting for my call, trying to set something up with Mary Carpenter, waiting, waiting…

If I could have talked to Mary Carpenter before this—only Mary—I was thinking, there would be a good chance. Without her—nothing.

Inside the old barn the rat smells blended with the fragrance of moldering hay and dung. I coughed. The little mechanic giggled again and stopped abruptly. It was dim at first, but I could make out shapes all right—the raised platform along the stalls, the overhead beam from which Esther Parrish had been hung upside down, the thick post supporting the beam, anchored to the raised ledge.

"Sit down," Bledsoe said.

He gave me a push toward the raised floor and I used the post to block and steady myself. I turned and sat on the edge of the shelf, shrugging, trying to accommodate the strain in my arms, the unaccustomed position.

"Now just take it easy," Bledsoe said. "Nothing to do but sit around. You can have something to eat when Bud gets back with the sandwiches."

I didn't say anything. I sat there with my feet barely touching the barn floor and felt time run past me like a fickle river. Sometimes it ran slow, sometimes fast, like a rapids, like Niagara Falls. But it kept running, because that is what time does, now and forever…

I was trying to guess what time it was when Bud came back with the groceries. Having nothing to check against, I could only try to feel it. But the thing about time is that you can't feel it. It doesn't stay long enough. It seemed as if we had been waiting for several hours, but it couldn't have been. Bledsoe and the little guy had found some old hay and made a couple of pallets on the barn floor. Bledsoe had taken out a pack of cards and for most of the time they had played pinochle. I hadn't watched anyone play pinochle for quite a while and it was something to look at. From time to time I shifted my position, moving my arms and my wrists tightly, to keep the circulation going. Each time I would move Bledsoe would look at me, watch till I settled down, then go back to his cards. The little mechanic kept giggling nervously. I developed a frantic urge to kick him in the mouth, but he was too far away across the barn floor. If he had been closer, I would have done it.

I heard the car stop in the barnyard and pretty soon Bud came in with a big paper sack under one arm, a gallon thermos in one hand, and a canvas picnic cooler in the other.

"Where the hell you been?" Bledsoe asked.

"Picking up the stuff," Bud said. "It's only three-thirty."

Bledsoe grunted, opened the paper bag, and looked into it.

"See the boss?" he asked.

"Yup," Bud said.

"Everything okay?"

"Yup."

"Okay, go put the car out of sight and come on back."

Bud went out. I heard the car for a short time, then silence and he returned.

Three-thirty, I kept thinking. Twelve hours till three-thirty again. Four and a half hours till eight o'clock in the morning.

"What about him?" Bud asked.

Bledsoe looked at me.

"Yeah," he said. "Give him a sandwich."

Bud dug a sandwich from the bag and started toward me, then stopped. "How's he going to eat it?" he said.

Bledsoe did some more looking, reached into his pocket, and came up with the key to the manacles. My heartbeat went crazy.

Now, I thought.

Bud came over to the ledge and laid the wrapped sandwich down beside me.

"Wait a minute," Bledsoe said. "I hear he's pretty handy."

He got on his feet and started looking around. I watched him stoop, scratch in the dirt, and pull up a length of thin cord. He came over to the ledge and I saw he had baling twine, thin, bristly. He tested it twice, yanking his hands outward, and it didn't break. He wrapped it around my neck, tied a knot, and I felt him doing something to one side at the post I was leaning against. He made an adjustment, and the thin cord came tight above my Adam's apple.

"Slipknot," he said. "The harder you pull, the tighter it gets."

"Yeah," I said.

"Okay, take the cuffs off him while he eats," Bledsoe said.

Bud knelt and fiddled around with the handcuffs, got them open, and slid my left wrist free. He left the thing locked on the other wrist. I sat very still, feeling the twine dig at my neck.

"Bottle of beer?" Bud said.

"Thanks," I said.

He went to the cooler and I picked up the sandwich and unwrapped it. It was a hamburger, with everything on it, generous size. I had no feeling of hunger, but when I took a bite of it, it was comforting. Besides, it would be silly not to eat. Strength is always better than weakness, always.

Bud flipped the cap off a bottle of beer and brought it to me. The dangling set of handcuffs made a musical sound as I drank. It was hard to swallow against the sharp twine, but it wasn't impossible. I ate very slowly and drank in sips. Bledsoe got through two sandwiches and two bottles before I had half finished. But it didn't bother anyone. There was no hurry about anything.

Bud got into the card game and they switched from pinochle to hearts, playing for a penny a point. The flat jangle of the coins on the floor was like an accompaniment to the jingling of the handcuffs as I would raise and lower the bottle. The beer was warm and tasteless before I finished.

The three of them were intent on the card game. I started to put the bottle down and saw that Bud had left the key to the manacles on the shelf, out of reach, the way I was strung up by the neck. If I could have leaned out only a little...

I sat there. I reached up and slid my fingers between my neck and the twine to loosen the noose. It would loosen all right, but that brought me closer to the post and farther from the key. I looked at the bottle in my left hand, slid my fingers between the twine and the post. I knew I could break it, but it would have to break the first time, just as the top of the bottle would break if all could be well timed.

Bledsoe glanced at me suddenly, but I had my hand away from the string, and after a moment he went back to the game. I looked at the key again. There was a crack in the boards of the ledge about three inches from where the key lay. The key had to be got rid of.

I leaned as far out as the noose would stretch and reached for the key with the bottle. I leaned a little farther, felt the slipknot draw up tight, the twine cut into my throat. I got the tip end of the bottle neck against the key and flipped it toward the crack. The thin key slid to the opening, fluttered, and disappeared. Bledsoe looked at me from one elbow. I got hold of the twine where it wrapped around the post, and as he started up, I yanked hard. My left arm went up and came down and the twine broke away from the post at the same moment the top of the bottle came off. Bledsoe was rushing at me, and behind him, Bud had started to move. I rolled back onto the ledge, turning, and managed to snap the open link of the manacles shut. They wouldn't be able to get that on me again.

I got on my feet as Bledsoe came up onto the ledge. I made a pass at him with the jagged end of the bottle, but he kept coming and I missed and went off balance. Bud was coming up at one side over my left shoulder. I straightened around and Bledsoe was on top of me. I shoved the glass into his belly, but it hit his belt buckle and slid off. Bud hit me on the back of the neck and I fell into Bledsoe's knees. He kicked up, straightening me. I felt Bud grab me from behind. I saw Bledsoe's overgrown fist coming but had no place to go. I had been hit harder in my time, but not much. As I fell I hung onto consciousness long enough to hear Bledsoe say:

"Pick him up and hold him…"

I didn't feel much then. I was getting sick to my stomach and I couldn't see. I felt an impact of about the intensity of a dentist's deep drill when the jaw is loaded with Novocain. It was only momentary. After that I felt nothing, nothing at all.

When I came around it was dark. Also it was cold. My head rang badly and felt as if it were split across the top. Some of my senses were working. I was lying in the stench of my own sickness and I got sick some more, then tried to move away from it. I could move, but I could go nowhere. There were boards behind me. I was curled up tightly, with boards at my head and feet, and when I blinked my eyes, I could see only the blankness of more boards. I thought about it for what seemed a long time and concluded that I was in one of the mangers in the stalls.

Where they found Peter that bad night, I thought. How much of Peter's life will I have to relive before zero hour?

I moved my hands and they worked all right. One of them was numb because I was lying on it. The manacles were still attached to my left wrist. I squirmed around, got a shoulder turned under me, stopped to rest, and squirmed some more. Meager light glowed above my head. I worked my way up, bracing myself with my feet against the end of the manger, twisted my neck, and looked through the crack. I could see across the raised platform to the main barn floor. A kerosene lantern burned dimly. Bledsoe was sitting up, drinking a bottle of beer. Beside him a smaller figure was stretched out, asleep. I couldn't find a third one.

After a while, after my head cooled from the heat of the first try, I raised up on my elbow. Pretty soon I could get my hand flat on the bottom of the cramped feedbox and I managed to straighten and lock my arm. I could see down a narrow passage that ran along the back of the open stalls, partitioned at the same height as the top edge of the manger. But there was nothing to see at the end but a solid wall. The entrance, where the cows had come in in days gone by, would be at the opposite end. I wasn't sure I could turn my bruised head far enough to see the opposite end.

I worked on it. I had to do some shifting and in the process learned that I wasn't tied anywhere. If I could keep the machinery working, I could move. It took a long time, but I got turned enough so that by straining in my neck I could look down the opposite direction to the stable door. Not that there was any visible door. I knew there had to be one, but a stack of ragged lumber and miscellaneous trash had been piled almost to the ceiling. Working my way through that would take about an hour and a half, without interruptions.

There would be interruptions.

There were always interruptions.

I settled down, resting on my elbows. The movement had helped, if only to confirm that it was a possibility. I couldn't figure out how to capitalize on it, but it was nice to know about. I concentrated on that niceness, trying not to think about what time it might be. I felt myself passing out, lowered my shoulders, and fought to stay conscious. There were some sounds out on the barn floor. I raised up enough to peer through the crack and saw Bledsoe on his knees, reaching for something. A bright flashlight gleamed in his hand and he got to his feet. I watched him approach, climb up onto the ledge and head toward the manger where I was lying...

The way Peter saw him coming that night, I thought.

Or so Peter had said.

I lay back again with my eyes closed, my hands loose on my drawn-up thighs. His footsteps thudded over the boards and the light shone down into the feed box. It flashed around, leaving my face. From under my nearly closed eyelids I saw him, bulky and battered, resting on his bare forearms on the edge of the manger. I saw the strap of his wrist watch, the glint of its face. But I couldn't read what time it was. He shone the light on me again and the last chance was on top of me. There wouldn't be another one, or anything easier.

The hand with the flashlight was deeper into the box than the other, also closer to me. I grabbed the wrist with both hands and when he pulled back in reflex yanked it down hard. He screamed as his elbow shattered on the plank above me. The flashlight fell on me and I hung onto his useless arm and clubbed him on the side of the head with the heavy-duty light. It was a good flashlight; it didn't go out. He was still struggling, his breath singing in his throat, trying to get at me with his good hand. I pulled myself onto my knees, hit him again in the head, and he sagged down against the feedbox. As I came over the edge onto the platform, the little mechanic was bustling up to see what had happened. I gave him the light in the face and he stopped.

"Where's Bud?" I said.

"Ain't here," he said. "Went back to town."

"You want to fight to hold me?"

"Uh—no," he said. "I got nothing against you. Never did have. The boss said—"

"All right. Is there a car here?"

"No, Bud took it."

My head was pounding badly and my eyes kept squeezing shut so that I had to keep forcing them open.

"What time is it?" I asked.

"I don't know."

"Go look at Bledsoe's watch."

He moved around me at a distance, watching me. I turned with his movement and watched him bend over, find Bledsoe's wrist, and look at the watch. Bledsoe groaned.

"Looks like his arm's broke," the mechanic said.

"I hope so," I said. "What time is it?"

"Four-thirty."

Four-thirty in the morning. How could he hit me hard enough to put me out for so long? I wondered.

The answer was easy. I had probably come around every so often and he had come over and tapped me again. Maybe eight, nine times. That was the way my head felt.

I couldn't think what to do with the scrubby little guy.

For that matter, I couldn't figure out what to do with Bledsoe.

Nothing, I thought. No time now. Do nothing. Leave him here. He won't go far.

"How far is it into town, across the fields?" I asked.

"About three miles in a straight line. Got to climb a few fences."

Three miles across the fields, climbing fences—about a forty-five-minute trip, I thought. That will make it five-fifteen in the morning, and I got to find Caroline Adams and Mary Carpenter. If I walk up to the Sampson farm, by the road, and use the telephone...

"Does Fred Sampson have a phone at his place?" I asked him.

"Uh—no. No, he don't. I tried to call him up about a tractor. He ain't got a phone."

"You know the nearest farm around here where there's a phone?"

"No. Some has got phones, but I don't know offhand without lookin' it up..."

It was a nothing idea anyway. The way I looked and smelled, with that set of manacles dangling from my wrist—nobody in his right mind would let me into the house, even if I could wake him up.

I flashed the light on Bledsoe and he was lying curled up, holding his broken arm gingerly, his eyes flicking now and then, not looking at anything.

"Bledsoe," I said, "you lie there and rest that arm. I'll look up a doctor and send him out to take care of it—after I get my chores done."

He didn't respond. I hadn't expected him to. I walked across the platform, got down on the barn floor, and started toward the open door of the barn. The little one scurried after me.

"What do you want me to do?" he said.

I flashed the light over him.

"I don't give a damn what you do. Stay here and keep Bledsoe company."

I started away again and he trotted at my heels.

"Listen, I didn't want to have nothing to do with this," he said, "kidnapping and all. I just—"

I stopped, lifted the flashlight, and he ducked back away from me.

"Just stay here," I said. "You can pour some beer down Bledsoe if he gets thirsty."

"Yeah—okay," he said.

I walked out of the barn, turned the corner of it, and started off in the direction of town. I hadn't gone forty paces when I came to a fence. I tossed the flashlight into the next field and started to climb. It was too rickety to climb. I kicked at the rotted post till it hung free, leaned against the rusty wire strands, and it folded down. I walked over it, picked up the light, and went on.

It was hard, lumpy walking. The field was plowed and had not been sown, and the clods were hard and unpredictable. I kept turning my ankles and sliding into holes between the rows of clumps. The only way I could navigate was by fixing a distant cluster of trees or the chimney of a far-off house and trying to maintain a steady line relative to them. Of course, they kept changing as I moved.

How did they navigate by the stars? I thought. And then I thought: The stars move at a different rate.

I thought about trying it with the stars, but it hurt too much to look up.

* * * *

I climbed twelve fences. Dogs barked at me a couple of times when I came too near the back of a farmhouse. Twice I had to duck down in a ditch and wait while a light went on, somebody yelled at the dog to shut up, the dog did, and the light went off.

On the last fence I had to make two tries. My legs were like dead tree trunks, and every step was a conscious effort to keep moving in spite of someone's trying to stick a knife in my groin. After I got over the fence, though, I saw a street light at a distance, and pretty soon I was on the sidewalk heading down into town.

My navigation hadn't been too bad. I came in on the back street, about a block up from the hotel and a block down, roughly at the corner where the beer joint opened off the alley. It wasn't open now.

I walked down the alley, turned the corner, and tried the door where Mr. Embers, the constable, had his office. There was a light burning, but nobody answered.

Quiet night, I thought.

CHAPTER 14

I sat down on the sidewalk with my back against the constable's door and rested. I began to pass out, the way I had back in the manger, and snapped my head from side to side to wake myself up. I decided my head would stay on all right, pushed myself up on my feet, and started up the street toward the hotel.

There was the sense of absolute desertion, the ghost-town feeling I'd had earlier—the day before—but intensified. My footsteps on the concrete walk made a fearful noise. Without thinking about it, I found myself walking faster, hugging the walls of the store fronts, fugitive and finished.

In one of the stores there was a clock on the back wall. I cupped my eyes with my hands and peered at it. Ten minutes past five.

Two hours and forty minutes to go, I thought.

If I called Sam, I thought, it may be a comfort—

But not to him, not unless I've got it wrapped in a bundle.

I looked up at the hotel door from the sidewalk.

When did I fall down? I wondered. I don't remember falling down.

After a minute I rolled onto my belly, got my hands under me, and pushed up. I climbed the steps one at a time, hanging onto the steel rail. The door was locked. I banged the screen. There was a light in the lobby, near the desk, but I couldn't see anyone. I banged some more. A door opened and there was more light. The young pimply-faced clerk peered out toward the door. I banged again. He came out of the office, around the desk, crossed the lobby in a leisurely way, and looked out at me. I rattled the doorknob. He stared at me, spread his arms, and shrugged.

He had solid orders, I decided. He couldn't let me in.

I shrugged back at him, took off my jacket, and wrapped it around my right hand. Holding the screen door open with my foot, I gave what I had left in the back and shoulders and put my padded fist through the window of the door. It made quite a lot of noise. The clerk jumped in the air and backward at the same time.

"Open the door," I said.

He waited till I had got my hand out of the jagged hole, then reached from some distance and turned a key. I kicked at the door and it swung open. He backed away as I entered.

"Got to see Miss Adams," I said.

"She's not in," he said.

"I'll go up and see."

I walked past him to the stairs and climbed up to the second floor. I was moving a little better than I had for a while.

You get closer, I thought, it's easier.

It took a couple of minutes of concentration to get the room numbers sorted out in my memory. I finally found my old room and counted my way down the hall to hers. I knocked. There was no answer. I knocked very hard and loud and still no answer.

She wouldn't do it, I thought. She wouldn't just run out.

I tried the knob and the door was locked. I put my shoulder against it and tried to force it, but it was an old, solid door and I didn't have the strength. Anyway, if she had heard me, she would by that time have responded.

I went back down the hall, down the stairs, and over to the desk. The clerk had disappeared, but the office door stood open and there was light beyond it. I walked around the desk and looked in there. The clerk was sitting at the desk, his hand on the phone.

"Made the call yet?" I asked.

"No."

"Don't bother with it. Miss Adams left me a message."

He did that spreading gesture with his hands. I started toward the desk. He got up on his feet and moved around to the far corner.

"Not that I know of—"

"Get me the message she left," I said.

He didn't move. I picked up the desk telephone and yanked on it, snapping the cord. When I set the instrument down, he moved around the desk and out to the lobby. I waited at his shoulder while he reached into a box and pulled out a folded slip of paper.

"Mac," it read. "It's four o'clock and I haven't heard from you. I called Jack Parrish and he said he had to talk to me about you and about Peter Davidian. It sounds like good news. I had Mary Carpenter invited to dinner, but I don't know—if I don't hear from you. I'm waiting to see Jack now." It was signed, "Caroline A."

I crumpled the note and dropped it on the floor. The clerk was watching me closely, the way a dog watches when it's waiting for you to wake up.

"You know Bud Carney?" I asked.

"Yeah—sure, I know Bud."

"Where does he live?"

He ran his tongue over his lips.

"Well, usually he stays with his folks, on the farm—"

"Where is he staying tonight?"

"He's—he came in—"

"What room is he in?"

"I don't remember."

I reached for him and he ducked.

"Honest," I said. "One more time."

"Third floor," he said quickly. "Number three-oh-one, at the head of the stairs."

"Give me a key."

"I can't—"

I lifted my hand. He ducked again, scurried to a board, and got a key. He had no way to know how useless the raised hand was.

Carrying the key, I climbed the three flights of stairs and came to Bud Carney's room. I didn't bother to be sneaky about it. When I had the door open and the light switched on, he was sitting straight up in bed, his fingers in his hairy chest. He didn't say anything, just looked at me.

"Where's my car?" I asked him.

"At Jack's," he said. "In the garage."

"Where are the keys?"

He nodded to one side.

"Over there, on the thing."

I went over and got them. They were the right keys.

"Is the garage locked?"

"Yeah—but—"

"But what?"

"It's an electric door. There's a switch under the beam on the right-hand side of the first door, facing west—first door from Main Street, I mean. You can't miss it."

"Okay," I said. "Go back to sleep."

I switched off the light, closed the door, and went away. As I crossed the lobby, the desk clerk, on a stool now, was bent over an open magazine, no longer watching.

"Good night," I said.

He didn't answer.

I went down the steps and across the street to the alley that led into Jack Parrish's International Harvester Distribution Franchise Station Dealership and Garage.

Whew! I thought.

As he had said, I couldn't miss the switch. The door lifted and the car was in there, sleek and powerful-looking. I unlocked the door, got under the wheel, and she started right away. It felt very fine. I backed it out into the alley, drove to the street, turned right, and headed for Jack Parrish's ranch house on the edge of town.

His sweeping drive was so accessible and so well-made that I turned off the lights and the engine as I hit it and drifted silently to a stop at his side entrance. When I got out, I left the car door open. His door was unlocked, as I had expected it to be. People don't lock doors in small towns. Hotels maybe…

It was an easy house to find the way around in. There was a big living room with some casual furniture and beyond that a den. I went into the den, turned on a light, and he had this big gunrack on the wall. Lots of guns, some antiques. There was an empty space in it. The gun that would have filled the space was lying on a desk in the middle of the room. A long-barreled, high-powered shotgun. I picked it up, put it under my arm, and found the stairs.

There was a broad upstairs hall running both ways from the staircase. I went to the first room, looked in, and it was empty. The next room was occupied and I went in quietly. Caroline Adams, fully dressed, was lying on the bed, her head on her arm, an afghan robe covering her to the waist. When I woke her she jumped, rolled away, and came up on both elbows, staring.

"Mac—"

"Everything's all right," I said. "We got to get busy. Which room is Parrish's?"

"I think it's at the end of the hall—that way." She pointed.

"My car's downstairs at the side door," I said. "Get yourself straightened up some and go down there. I'll be along."

"Yes," she said, pushing at the afghan. "Listen, Mac, I don't know how it happened. I didn't hear from you—"

"Forget it," I said. "You didn't have any choice. Just go down to the car and get in the back seat."

She nodded and I went to the hall and turned down toward the end. When I opened the door, Jack Parrish's voice said, "What is it?"

He was half asleep. I switched on the light and said, "Come on, get up."

He got up fast then. He was halfway across the room before he saw the gun under my arm. He stopped. He was wearing pajama bottoms, no tops. The pulse in his beefy neck was going hard like a trapped bird's pulse.

"Get your clothes on," I said. "We got to make a call."

He stared at me, opened his mouth, closed it, looked at the gun, turned away, and picked up a pair of pants.

On a bedside table sat a small electric alarm clock. The time read six-oh-five. I could be fairly sure it was correct. I picked up the clock and turned it over. It was set for seven forty-five. That would give him fifteen minutes to get waked up, maybe have a cup of coffee. At this distance from Stateville, unfortunately, he wouldn't have the extra thrill of watching the momentary dimming of the lights.

He went into a big walk-in closet and I sat on the edge of the bed, waiting. Pretty soon I became aware that he was stalling on me. When I looked at the clock, it read six-fifteen.

If ten minutes can pass so fast, I thought, we'll have to get jumping.

"Let's go," I said into the closet.

I got up and he looked out. He was buttoning a shirt, slowly.

"May I ask...?" he said.

That didn't sound like him.

"The hell with it," I said. "Just come on."

He came out from behind some hanging suits of clothes and he had this handgun, low, near his hip. I saw it before he could lift it. I squeezed off on the shotgun and he started dancing. It sounded as if the house had caved in. Suddenly from downstairs Caroline Adams was calling shrilly:

"Mac—answer me—are you all right?"

"Drop the gun," I said.

Parrish dropped it.

"I'm all right," I called. "Get in the car."

Parrish kept staring at me.

"Well, move," I said.

He turned and left the room, and I followed him downstairs and out to where the car was parked. Caroline Adams was in the back seat.

"Slight change of plans," I said. "You feel up to driving?"

"Of course," she said.

"Okay, good. Mr. Parrish and I will ride in the back seat."

She got out, opened the front door, and got under the wheel. I nodded to Parrish.

"You first," I said.

He gave me a look, bent, and climbed in.

"All the way, please."

He moved to the far corner of the seat. I got in on the near side with the gun on my knees and my thumb on the trigger.

"Drive to the Carpenters'," I said.

"The…?" Miss Adams said.

"Got to talk to Mary Carpenter," I said. "No more time to do it the convenient way. It's after six o'clock, not too early to get somebody up."

She was driving the big car smoothly along the street. It was getting light now and the trees were still and graceful in the dawn. The Carpenter house sat high in silhouette from the lower level of the street. She turned in there, drove to the side-porch entrance, and stopped.

"Will you go in and get her up and dressed?" I said to Miss Adams. "She'll have to hurry."

"Of course."

She left the car. I looked at Jack Parrish, who was sitting on the far side of the seat, staring straight ahead.

"What the hell is going on?" he said.

"I don't want to go over everything twice," I said. "Just relax. You know the gun better than I do, but I know how to use it. I wouldn't shoot you, of course, unless you move something, like your finger or toe. I'm jumpy and I'm in a hurry. Don't trust me."

He sat there.

It was stuffy in the car and I was having to fight to stay awake, as before. I pushed a button and the automatic window rolled down. The fresh air helped. But I wished my head would stop buzzing.

Caroline Adams came from the house, leading Mary by the hand. The girl looked sleepy and puzzled. When she got into the seat beside Miss Adams, she stared into the back seat and after a minute she said:

"Hello, Mr. Parrish."

"Hello, Mary," he said.

He didn't move anything except his mouth.

Miss Adams drove onto the street and stopped.

"Drive out north of town, to the old Davidian farm," I said.

She looked around quickly, hesitated, then pushed a button and got started. Parrish started to turn his head, thought better of it and sat still, facing front.

The town was coming to life as we reached the main corner and swung onto the road leading north. The few people on the street glanced at us and glanced away.

Not much interest on Monday morning, I thought.

"Mary," I said, "we were talking the other day about the time Peter Davidian fixed the tire for Esther's car and was going to change it, you remember, and he had to go pick up another jack and Esther went with him—"

After a while she said, "I remember."

"Will the car go any faster?" I asked Miss Adams. She pushed it and we moved faster, going out of town.

"And you got tired of waiting," I said, "and left the car. And somebody came along and gave you a ride."

"Yes."

"Who?"

"I told you—Tony Bledsoe. He was out somewhere working on a tractor and came by."

"So Tony Bledsoe gave you a ride home. And you told him what had happened about the flat tire?"

"Well, sure—"

"And you told him Esther had gone with Peter to the Sampson farm and hadn't got back yet, forty-five minutes later—"

"I—guess—"

"Did you tell him that?"

"Yes, I guess I told him that."

"Did he say anything about that?"

"Did he…? I don't remember."

"Would he be likely to say something about it? Or was it a matter of maybe he would and maybe he wouldn't?"

"I don't know what you mean."

"Did Tony Bledsoe come in the gas station downtown while you were waiting for the tire to be fixed?"

"He—I don't—well, I guess he did."

"He was there when Esther was teasing Peter about marrying him and all that?"

"Well—she was talking, like she did—"

"So Tony Bledsoe would have heard that too."

"I don't know—"

"What difference would it have made to Tony?"

"How do I know? No difference."

"No difference?"

Jack Parrish turned his head. I didn't shoot him. I looked at him and I was glad to have the gun.

"Tony told you that Peter drove into the garage the day before," I said, "and warned him that something would happen to Esther if you didn't look out."

He stared at me.

"Peter never did that," I said. "Tony made that up. Didn't it ever occur to you that if he had told you about it right away you would have done something? He didn't tell you till it was too late."

His mouth tightened and spread, and the little muscles jumped around.

"Mary," I said, "Esther and Tony Bledsoe were kind of—going together, weren't they?"

"Going to—Tony Bledsoe—?"

"Yeah."

The car swerved as Caroline Adams slowed suddenly and made the turn onto the country road. Ahead I could see the small sprawl of the abandoned farm.

"That's silly," Mary said.

"Silly but true," I said. "And you covered up for them, didn't you?"

"No—I—"

We slowed abruptly and made the turn into the rutted lane. The car bounced and shifted heavily. A few feet short of the barn door it came to a stop. I opened the door, got out, and nodded at Parrish.

"Come on in the barn," I said. "I think you'll be interested."

Caroline Adams was sitting behind the wheel and Mary Carpenter had her face in her hands.

"Please come in," I said. "Won't take long. It's fairly important."

"All right, Mary," Miss Adams said. "Come on. You'll be all right."

I was explaining to Parrish as we strolled into the barn.

"As I already said to Miss Adams," I said, "Peter believed he really did kill Esther. He and Esther were fooling around, kid fashion, in the front room of the Sampson house, and he got aroused and she decided to quit—the way those things go—and he slammed out of the house, went to change the tire, and when he went to pick her up, she wasn't there, so he drove on into town and had something to eat. He said other things—he said he hit her and she fainted; he said somebody came up on the front porch. He made up a lot of things because, when he told the story straight at first, nobody would believe him, not even his own lawyer, and he had a big guilt thing about fooling with her and then he had the shock of discovering her murdered in this barn..."

We were inside now. Tony Bledsoe was sitting on the edge of the platform, his broken arm resting on his thigh, his head in his propped hand. He didn't look at us.

"But some of what Peter said couldn't have been true, even to my knowledge," I said to Parrish. "There isn't any front porch on the Sampson house for anybody to come up on. He would tell me, wildly, how would I know or care whether there was a porch or not. Another thing he said was that when they found him in the barn, there was a rush toward him and Tony Bledsoe was coming after him. Couldn't be. Tony wasn't with the posse—with you and the sheriff and the others. He was hanging around the hotel downtown."

Off to one side, Caroline Adams and Mary Carpenter were standing just inside the barn door. Tony Bledsoe looked up from his hand, his eyes shot with pain.

"Jack," he said, "you bring a doctor?"

Parrish didn't say anything.

"Tony had been here earlier, though," I said. "Before the posse. With Esther."

Bledsoe moved jerkily, then tightened and sat still. Parrish's jaw muscles were writhing around his teeth.

"When Mary told him that Esther had gone off with Peter to the Sampson place, she hit a hot nerve in Tony Bledsoe. He drove Mary home, took about five minutes, drove back to the Sampson place, and was in time to catch Esther and Peter fooling around. Peter left and Tony went in. And that's enough details. The main thing is, Peter Davidian didn't kill Esther. Tony Bledsoe killed her."

Bledsoe looked up again, hunted this time, looking for a place to go. He started up off the ledge and Parrish broke. He made a sound like a startled bird and charged at the man with the broken arm. I watched them, the gun cradled in my arm. Mary Carpenter ran from the barn, screaming. Then Tony Bledsoe screamed. A hand clutched at my sleeve and I looked at Caroline Adams.

"Mac—please!" she said. "Don't let him—"

I woke up somehow, squeezed off on the big gun. The fight stopped. Parrish reeled off to one side. Tony Bledsoe was lying on his good arm, gasping for breath. The last thing I remember about that barn was the wrinkled face of the scrawny mechanic peering over the edge of the manger, where he had tried to hide. It was a bad place to hide. Some of us could have told him.

Outside, Mary Carpenter was leaning on the hood of the car, her face in her arms. Caroline Adams was trying to comfort her.

"Parrish!" I called.

He came out of the barn, unsteady on his feet.

"I got to get to a phone," I said. "You drive, huh? Then you can drop me off and get a doctor or cop or something to come for Bledsoe. Get a cop. Better that way."

Caroline Adams helped Mary into the back seat and got in beside her. I got in with Parrish and he backed the car onto the road, turned, and headed for town. He didn't waste any time. We didn't have any conversation and it was all right with me.

I got Sam Birch on the phone at twenty minutes past seven. At that time, at Stateville, they were working over Peter Davidian, being gentle about it, gentle, but inexorable. Sam plugged me into the connection so I could hear him talk to the governor and what the governor said in reply.

"The Davidian boy is innocent and we know who killed Esther Parrish," Sam said. "I can have it on paper for you sometime today."

"All right, Mr. Birch," the governor said. "I'll call the warden. Nice going."

"Thank you, sir," Sam said.

"Thanks for letting me listen," I said.

"Don't mention it," Sam said. "Call me up when you get back to town and we'll have a drink."

"That would be nice."

I hung up and went outside. Caroline Adams was leaning against the doorway of the constable's office where Parrish had taken me to make the call.

"Thanks for everything," I said. "Sorry about the melodrama and stuff. There was the time squeeze—and I had to do it strong enough to break Bledsoe down a little in front of Parrish. I had to have witnesses."

"Don't apologize," she said. "There's only one thing—I'm sure Mary had no idea that Tony would actually kill Esther."

"I'm sure she didn't too," I said. "In fact, right at the moment, only two people know it for certain, Tony Bledsoe and me. But I have a hunch he'll let some others in on it before the day is over."

We stood there for a moment in the morning sun.

"*Parlez-vous francais?*" I said.

"*Oui...*"

"*S'il vous plâit*—have breakfast with me?"

She smiled.

"Any time," she said. "Any time at all, when you're free."

I took her hand and we started up the street toward the Wesley Café.

"Do you speak French, really?" she said.

"No, uh-uh," I said. "No, I don't. I speak Chicago."

Her hand moved in mine as we started to cross the street. It was a good hand. She was a good girl. I never saw her again after that time in Wesley.

www.ingramcontent.com/pod-product-compliance
Lightning Source LLC
Chambersburg PA
CBHW020653180626
46816CB00003B/1255